A New Odyssey

Frank Hughes, Jr.

Llumina Press

ISBN: 978-1-59526-707-8

Printed in the United States of America by Llumina Press

Library of Congress Control Number: 2007903083

For Kat

*Having you in my life fills my heart with love more
and more everyday.*

Chaos, simple.

In the beginning there were only three: Fire, Rock, and Water. They ran wild. Crashing, smashing, and splashing all over each other, with no regards for the consequences. It was irreverent, irresponsible and fun to be so simple, straight and predictable. Fire was hot, consuming everything, following its agenda. Rock was massive, always present but never overbearing. Water was omnipresent, able to subdue Fire's intensity, complement Rock's integrity.

To watch them play, you would think they were out to destroy each other. Fire would ravish Rock, Water would evaporate Fire, Rock would swallow Water. The fact of the matter is that Rock knew Fire burnt, Fire knew Water extinguished, and Water knew Rock was everchanging. They understood each other, and Chaos, happy Chaos reigned supreme. Until... Life.

When no one was looking, Life quietly emerged. Small at first, it grew amongst the Chaos. The three friends certainly didn't seem to mind—they even toned down their act so Life could flourish. For millions of years Fire, Rock, Water, and Life existed happily together. From time to time a little rough play ensued, but for the most part all was fine. And just as it is true today, so it was back then: when everything seems fine and dandy, BOOM, an asteroid slams into your planet. The collision ignited Fire, erupted Water, and shook Rock. So disoriented were these three friends, they went on a rage that nearly destroyed the entire planet, and all Life thereon. Life's only rescue from the fury was Time. And, in time, things settled down, but not before the majority of Life was erased, leaving only small pockets here and there. And Chaos took its toll.

As the years passed, the scars of the impact slowly healed and Life re-emerged in force, this time bent on conquering the planet, led by man (and woman). Millennia of evolution, volumes of literature, archives of art, and miles and miles of cultural heritage all accumulated and progressed to one thing. Me.

I'm Ulysses, and everything that transpired before now in not just human or planetary history, but universal history, has done so just so I can stand at a subway station and wait for a train to take me to the same place it does every day. How fulfilling.

Frank Hughes, Jr.

Okay, so maybe all history wasn't dedicated to my benefit, but sometimes it feels like a lot of weight falls on my shoulders. I'm three years out of school, Flagler College, and work at a small bank in Boston. I take the train into work every day, so I'm saving a ton of miles every year on my new car. I have two options when it comes to a train station: Main Street Station, which is close to my apartment, but its downtown location is a bit dangerous, and Bailey Park Station, which is in the middle of a snobby little town where everyone wears an ascot, drives a German SUV, and every wife/soccer mom at one time held a title that started "Miss" and required a sash.

I know it doesn't seem like a difficult decision, but if you break it down from my point of view, then you'll understand why I pick door number one: Main Street. Why, you ask? Can you say leggy blond with dimples, a great smile, and likes the Red Sox?

She takes the train to work the same time I do. One day I overhear a conversation she is having with some guy. He's tall, well-groomed, well-dressed: obviously gay. He does a lot of the talking, something about work and his boss and how important he is but no one recognizes it, and that the company will fall apart if he left. Presumably with his gay lover.

I get off at South Station; she gets off sometime after that. I'm not sure where exactly, but one day last October, she was wearing a Fenway Park staff jacket and talking about the playoffs. Down the line is Park Street; she could catch the Green line to Kenmore. How cool would it be if she worked at Fenway Park? There's something about girls who like baseball, but if they work in one of the holiest places ever created by man—Fenway Park—well, the very thought brings a tear to my eye.

I remember this Monday morning a few months ago. It was your typical gloomy Monday, dark clouds, drizzle, cold; then she showed up and the clouds seemed to part, as if to allow a little sun to dance through her golden hair. Maybe I'm embellishing a bit, but wow, can she make an entrance. She smiled that day, just as we both reached the train door. I stopped to let her go. The best part was that her friend was not around. Clearly, he was home with his boyfriend.

It's tough to be twenty-five years old and have a stupid crush on someone you don't know, and will never know.

7:35 am. The train should be arriving within 5 minutes or so, and

2

no mystery girl today. I've nicknamed her "Ranger-girl." I hate being so impersonal, calling her "that girl," or "her," not that Ranger-girl is very flattering. One day she stood at the station with boots. Cowboy boots. She obviously didn't like them. You could tell they hurt her undoubtedly cute little feet when she walked. But she walked like a cowboy, put it together: walks like a cowboy, cowboys are from Texas, the Texas Rangers, Walker, Texas Ranger, Ranger-girl. Think what you will, the entire male population of North Union Bank, and several "in-the-know" females, refer to this mystery girl as Ranger-girl. I've never seen the boots since.

People are gathering quickly as the anticipation of the train, and going to work, builds. Suddenly, there's Ranger-girl. Today she's sporting a blue, floral one-piece dress with a solid blue sweater. As always, her backpack is around one shoulder and her purse strap cuts across her chest. Oh, what a chest. She can't be more than a B cup. Definitely not a C. Maybe a BB? Is there such a size as BB? The purse strap bisects her breasts perfectly. Her sandy-blond hair is up in a ponytail, she must have slept late today. Oh, man those are great breasts. "Oh, shit…"

She just caught me checking her out. A twenty-five year old banker just got caught by the nameless girl he's infatuated with. Moron. She hasn't acknowledged the indiscretion; maybe I'm okay. Maybe I was looking for the train. Yeah, looking for the train twelve feet away in the middle of her chest. Tomorrow I'll choose door number two.

Mercifully, the train arrives, and all enter. Ranger-girl and I get in the same car from different ends. However, we both gravitate towards the middle like sheep in a box car.

"I'm not looking over, I'm not looking over," I mutter. A little Asian woman hears me. "I am so choosing door number two tomorrow." With a slight grin and a shake of the head, I regain my composure. I mean, for the love of God, I call her Ranger-girl. Time to justify things—I should look at her breasts. I'm a man. I was raised by Jack Tripper on *Three's Company*. Men always check out women—it's the ritual, it's expected. That gives the sign to the women to come and claim the men. Show a little interest, maybe a conversation will start up, and from there who knows. I'm just a person, she's just a person, we should talk.

"Ah-chewwww."

What was that? Oh my goodness, she sneezed. If only I could bless her, but unfortunately, that would not be my job. She's too far away, on a crowded train. She's expecting those within one or two bodies to bless her. Why don't they bless her, don't these people have mothers? Heaven forbid someone show a bit of human courtesy on the train! Okay, if I can make eye contact, I can send her a silent blessing, mouth the words. That would be cute; she'd remember me as the nice guy who blessed her, after staring at her breasts.

"I'm one step from being a stalker." The Asian woman looks at me again.

The moment is gone. She probably doesn't even remember sneezing anymore. The remainder of the ride is uneventful. I get off at South Station, and Ranger-girl continues on. As the doors close behind me, I put my shoulders back, fix my tie, and walk towards the stairs, on my way to work. "Door number two it is...."

Every day is the same thing. I commute

seven minutes by car; I wait for, and check out my mysterious not-quite-yet, never-will-be girlfriend; I get a coffee from this great little diner just outside the train station called Uncle Charlie's; twenty-five minutes on the train, then walk a block and a half to my building; finally, struggle to find my ID badge. I know it is always in my wallet, but for some reason I feel compelled to check every pocket on my person before I think of checking my wallet. Shirt pockets—empty. Front pants pockets—change from my coffee on the left, lucky rock on my right. Yes, I carry a lucky rock everywhere I go. Why? Beats the hell out of me, but a while back a friend of mine gave it to me, telling me it was lucky. Apparently these rings that run through and around the surface of this particular rock store luck for whoever carries it. Ever since hearing that I've been afraid to part with it, after all it's only as big as a bottle cap. Has it brought me luck? Beats me, but if I'm living a charmed life now, I don't need to know what will happen without the rock.

Monrow & Midder of Philadelphia built the old Armstrong building back in 1871. I know this because every day, while searching for my ID badge, I focus on the stupid plaque that reads "Monrow & Midder, 1871." I was fortunate enough to be exploring my person one day last summer, hunting for my ID badge while some architecture students from BU, or someplace, were examining the building. They weren't allowed in, so they asked me a couple of questions about the inside. They wanted to know about door jams, windowsills, and floorboards. Apparently, Security wouldn't let them look around, so they hustled us idiots who couldn't find their ID badges, sharing information along with their barrage of questions. That day I learned that Monrow & Midder were from Philadelphia and that the building had been on fire twice but never destroyed. I followed that observation with "twice, and never destroyed, no kidding…" They missed my sarcasm. For a while after that I was pretty good about finding my ID badge before getting to the building, but lately I've reverted back to my old habits.

With a swipe, and a green light, I'm in the door. Immediately to the right is the security desk. In the morning it's usually manned by two men, Clint and Charles. Not their names, I don't know what their real

5

names are, but if Clint Eastwood and Charles Bronson ever worked private security for a corporation, these guys would be them. On the day of the "Architecture Incident," as it later became known, these two blowhards gave me a hard time for divulging sensitive information to a couple of "beatniks," as Clint referred to them. These two sorry old farts love giving everyone a hard time, as if this is their building, and they decide who should be allowed in and who is not worthy. Hell, they were probably alive when the damn thing was built. "Good morning, gentlemen, I trust all is well?" I asked. I try every day to be less and less sincere, hoping to provoke one of them to yell at me again. But they are good.

"Good morning, young man, how are you?" casually asks Clint while standing in front of the security desk. He's got some kind of chain he's rolling between his fingers; I'd guess rosary beads or dog tags. Clint is the only one of the two ever to talk. Charles just sits. If a situation arises, Charles will take his walkie-talkie off his belt, but it's rare. I think every day Clint tries to say his good morning nicer and nicer just to provoke me. He's a worthy adversary.

"I am very well, thank you, enjoying everything the day has to offer right now." Clint opens his mouth to continue our conversation, but no words exit. He just stands there solemn and still. My first reaction is to ask is he is having a heart attack, but just as I get ready to step forward he turns to Charles and excuses himself for a minute. Charles and I exchange a quick glance; I smile and head off to the elevators. That was odd, I wonder if I'll be crazy when I get old.

The elevators are slow. So very slow. Most days I hit the button and think about why I'm not taking the stairs. Laziness is usually the answer; maybe I have walking mono. Can you have walking mono? Okay, I'm just lazy. The trick with the elevator is not about being the first one on, but the first one at the controls. That way you decide who gets on, and who waits. Some days, when I need to be by myself, it's a quick "Close Door", but most days I'm willing to let others join me, especially if they're cute.

One day I get on with this other guy. We claim our corners, careful not to make eye contact. Just as the doors close, a hand dives between them. A large hand. Fingers the size of baby arms. The doors split open again, as if it had any other option, and a hulk of a man walks in. He had to be seven feet tall, well over three hundred pounds. My eyes

6

darted to the weight allowance sticker. I think we had a pound or two to spare. He lumbers in, turned, and reaches for the buttons to select his floor. I can actually hear the cables tightening above our heads. Just as he's about to hit three he turns, looks at me and the other guy, starts to laugh and says, "Hey, we're all going to the third floor. We're the third floor club!" After a brief second, we both realized that no matter how lame this guy was, his size demands a polite laugh. We laugh, the doors close, and the "third floor club" ascends to our pre-destined location. Unfortunately, that was the last meeting of the club. I took the stairs for nearly a week, a record that shall never be broken.

When we hit the third floor, that moment between the elevator dinging and the door opening is quite a moment of clarity for me. Actually, it's a lot like that moment just after you have sex with either someone you don't like or someone you shouldn't be having sex with and you think, "Is this right?" Just before that door opens I think, "Is this right? Should I be here? Didn't I have higher goals for myself, loftier ambitions? What is it that pulls me here every day, after successfully escaping every night?" Before I know it, I'm at my desk. My voice-mail light is on, my e-mails are filtering in, and all the crap I left last night is right where I left it. At least I have a good view, my exotic-island calendar. I got it in last year's Christmas grab. Some days I just stare at palm trees in Maui and think, I could be doing this there. Of course, I'd probably be sitting at a desk in Maui, looking at a calendar of snow falling on the Paul Revere statue in Boston, longing for a New England winter.

Today is September 13th. Monday. 8:30 am. After a long pause, trying to contemplate that significance, I decide it's time for a muffin. A blueberry muffin. A quick look across the floor and there they are, Jonathan and Flip, my two best friends since high school. Jonathan has this thing about his name; he doesn't like to be called any variation of it. No John, or Johnny, or Jack, or John-boy: nothing except Jonathan. Flip's real name is Fredrick. Fredrick Lawrence Paine, F.L.P...Flip. Ever since I first met him, he has been Flip. I didn't know that wasn't his real name until four years ago, when I went with him to get his license renewed on his twenty-first birthday and he had to sign everything Fredrick. Most people never get to learn his real name, they just call him Flip and that's that. We all work for the same company, but we've all taken different routes here. I'm the manager of a mutual-fund custodian group that North Union manages, Triple B Home Life. The title sounds good, but it's still a step or two from respectability. Flip does the same stuff, but at assistant manager level, meaning same responsibility, less pay. And Jonathan…well, he works in human resources. HR, in many companies, is like the strict assistant principals we all had in junior high. You don't know they exist until they knock on your cube and tell you that someone has a problem with what you did, said, wrote, joked, or thought. Your boss is your boss, they have a boss, and they have a boss and so on and so forth, there's a protocol, a hierarchy. But HR, they can be a bunch of pricks if someone not too friendly to you gets to them first. They don't care if you are vice-president of corporate infrastructure or vice-president of manila folder distribution. If they hear any story that could look bad in the press, or cause a lawsuit, you are screwed. Guilty until proven guiltier, you never get the benefit of a trial, or the chance to face your accuser. I've seen it happen. Very uncool.

We had this one guy, Dwayne Martinez; he was older, a father, really friendly. Everyone loved him, except Kristen and Donna. You see, Dwayne was in his late fifties, father of five girls. FIVE GIRLS. Considering Junior, Senior, and friends' proms, that is a minimum of 15 prom nights. That's over one hundred thousand dollars in weddings. It's getting up three hours early just to get to the bathroom before work, every day. If that was me, I'd kill myself. Natural family planning my ass, there's nothing natural about five daughters within eight years of each other. Poor Dwayne.

Well anyway, being a nice guy, but a little too touchy/feely, Dwayne always puts his hands on your back. Man, woman, older, younger, superior, or underling. These two, shall we say women, didn't like it. So instead of telling Dwayne, they went to HR. Two weeks later, Dwayne was told he was being transferred to another group. He was told it was because he made someone feel uncomfortable. Bitches. He was just being a nice guy. He only worked here to keep busy: Dwayne had saved a lot of money from shrewd real-estate maneuvers. He did his job—better, I might add, than most everyone else in the group, including Kristen and Donna. He didn't look for promotion, just a fair raise every year, and the companionship of other friendly people.

No one knew what happened, just that one day Dwayne was called into a meeting, and an hour later, looking a little broken up, he packed

A New Odyssey

his desk and moved one floor up. A couple of days later he told some of the guys in the group a little of what happened, rightly thinking that it was probably a woman (or so DNA might prove) that ratted him out. I did a little poking around through my connections in HR (Jonathan) and found out that Kristen and Donna were the two rats. Jonathan didn't actually come out and tell me, but he didn't deny it was those two. I kept this information to myself for a day or two; I wanted to really verify what I could. You see, the two of them have been in the bank for a long time, they apparently met here, how romantic. Neither finished college, both started in the mailroom. In eight years, they had gotten to a level some people start at right out of school.

Now I'm not saying they're stupid, but there is so much you learn in college that supplements your education, like teamwork, communication, and expression. Add on that these two were live-in, love-in, peanut-butter-lickin', dog-faced, butch-hair, I-never-wear-skirts lesbians, and you've got quite a recipe for ignorance. I know gay people. In college, I was very involved with the theater, and I had a girlfriend that was an art major. Many of our closest friends were gay, but they weren't assholes. Kristen and Donna are your typical man-hating lesbians. No one ever asked, no one ever pried, no one really cared, but now they made things personal. They almost got one of the nicest guys in the world fired, and for what? A man who probably knows as much, if not more, about women than these two touches one of them harmlessly on the back, and they freak.

Kristen and Dwayne had worked together for about a year before Donna started in our group. I think Donna was jealous of Dwayne touching Kristen. We all believe Donna is the more masculine of the relationship, if not the uglier. Not three weeks after Donna started, Dwayne was transferred.

If I were dating say, Ranger-girl (I've got to get her name), I could not work in the same group with her. It's inappropriate. But I didn't pass judgment right away; I sat back and watched these two at work. I kept the knowledge of Kristen and Donna to myself. I didn't want the group to pick sides; I didn't want a civil war. I like my job, and I'll protect everyone I can from this point on. Dwayne was just a casualty of office war. I've pulled everyone in the group aside, including Kristen and Donna so they wouldn't feel left out, and reminded them that work is for work. Before work, after work and lunch is yours, but within these walls, just do your

9

work. Later I talked to them, separately of course, and I ended the meeting with, "…do your work, and don't let too many people in on your business," and this was the dinger, "not that you have to worry about anything at all. Your business is your business." With that, I tried to say everything is cool, I know the score, and I'm okay with whatever you have going on. I'm on your side. As God is my witness, I'll lull them into a false sense of confidence, and WHAM, I'll get them both canned. I'll be revered as the man who dispatched the evil, hetero-phobic lesbians.

I need my muffin.

It's the same thing every morning; the first two in find each other, usually Flip and Jonathan, and we wait for the third, usually me. Unless we are being audited, it's rare that anyone is in before 8:50 am. The three of us go to cafeteria and stand by the windows to look at all the people filing in, either pointing out the ones we want to sleep with, or the ones we think it would be funny if one of the others slept with. We try to be quiet; a lesbian could be anywhere.

Last fall, Jonathan got married. He and his wife Dany tried to have kids right away, but she miscarried after 10 weeks. He doesn't talk much about it, but sometimes I think that if all went well, he'd be a father right about now. If I'm thinking about it, then I'm sure he is, but you'd never know. It's led to some hard times for the two of them. She's afraid to get pregnant again, and who could blame her, but he thinks that trying will ease the suffering. Jonathan has stayed over my apartment a couple of times after arguing with Dany. I hope they don't divorce; he'd be devastated. They've been together for ten years. In high school, everyone was so jealous of him. We all wanted Dany; I remember begging my parents to get a pool just to see her come over in a bathing suit. I never had a shot with her; I had bad skin, and every day was a confidence battle. Flip liked her too, but he was way too weird in high school for any girl to take him seriously. At least my skin cleared up—Flip's still whacked.

It's funny, even though Jonathan and Dany went out for years, since they were sophomores in high school, they actually waited two years before they had sex for the first time, which I think is exceptional. At the time, I thought Jonathan was a faggot, but looking back, he did things right. Though he'd never admit it then, he was in love. How do I know he was in love? He never bragged about the sex. In ten years, I have discovered that Dany likes being on top, wears red boots when she is in the mood, and still owns a cheerleader uniform for only one reason. Jonathan is very tight-lipped about the rest. He keeps the intimate moments to himself. Sometimes, when the planets are in perfect alignment and either Flip or I have memorable sexual encounter, we'll tell each other and Jonathan. But even the wildest sex does not get a raise out of Jonathan, as if he's been there and done that. Flip and I are sure Jonathan goes to bed with a big smile on his face more often then not.

Jonathan is planning a surprise first anniversary party for Dany at the same restaurant as their wedding reception. It's not going to be any big celebration, just family and close friends. I think the planning and secrecy of the party helps distract him from their recent problems. Flip has also been into the planning stages of another celebration, a kind of reunion. Unfortunately, he needs both Jonathan and I to pull it off.

"OK, I'll ask you one more time," Flip says, "because I've got to figure out how we'll get there: two doors, four doors, or minivan"?

"No, not again?" Jonathan is quick to reply.

I just kept eating my muffin, pretending to be fixated on someone, or thing, outside.

"Look," Flip starts, "it's like, a thousand miles, and I'll do all the driving. This girl wants me, but I can't show up alone, I'll look like an idiot."

Silence.

"We leave Wednesday after work, we arrive around 2 am, get a hotel room, twelve hours later we eat the biggest turkey we've ever seen. You guys take the car, I stay the night there, Friday you pick me up, and we go to New York Saturday. We'll be home for football on Sunday."

More silence.

"C'mon, guys," Flip pleads, adding that this will complete one of the items on our top ten list of things to do in a lifetime.

For a moment, Jonathan and I look at each other and try to think what item traveling to Minnesota would be categorized as. Collectively we came up with 10 items and/or accomplishments that would lead to a fulfilling life. From high school to college to now, we've made a few amendments to the list, like replacing a date with Pam Anderson to just hooking up with a celebrity. Fine tuning over the years, if you will.

11

Here is top ten list, in no particular order:
1. Hook up with a celebrity.
2. Catch a baseball at Fenway Park.
3. Give a presentation at work while not wearing pants.
4. Be in either a TV commercial or opening sequence to a TV show.
5. Sing the National Anthem before any sporting event.
6. Strip at a bachelorette party for cash.
7. Complete a perfect football season playing Madden on Play-Station.
8. Have a story (a true story) that either starts or ends with the phrase, "I was making out with twins."
9. Get a friend so drunk that they can be toilet-papered from head to toe like a mummy.
10. Punch Bryant Gumbel (why Bryant Gumbel? Why not?)
There is another item, we call it 10a. Find happiness.

Yes, we know that technically we have eleven items, but that last one, 10a, is subjective. To tell the truth Dany made us add it after finding out we had a list. She insisted that it would aid in our development and maturity into manhood.

So far Flip has done the best, actually getting five things accomplished. He has given not one, but two presentations with his pants down by his ankles (#3). He was in the parking lot of a furniture store when they were filming a commercial and got into a wide shot they show all the time on TV (#4). He has stripped at a bachelorette party, granted he was not asked, but he did take in four dollars (#6). He and I share the next one, both of us completing perfect seasons, 19-0, playing Madden on PlayStation (#7). Jonathan has not attempted this item, but then again Jonathan has a woman and gets laid while Flip or I are playing video games. All three of us have gotten one another so trashed that mummification in toilet paper was very easy (#9). I actually was able to wrap both Jonathan and Flip together; that made for a great Christmas card.

Individually, I've caught a ball at a Red Sox game (#2). It was hit by none other than Rod Carew when he was with the Angels. I was ten and he was hitting batting practice and I remember dropping the ball, but I was the first to pick it back up. Jonathan says he found that happiness crap (#10a), but he has to say that it's his wife's contribution to the list. Dany would kill him if he wasn't completely and utterly happy. She'd also kill him if he accomplished numbers 1, 3, 6, 8 or 10. Jonathan gets credit for two accomplishments, but Flip and I always note an asterisk when referring to his life.

So Flip wants to justify a Minnesota road trip as possibly fulfilling a top ten lifetime accomplishment. After reviewing the list, I just don't see where that would fit in. She's not a celebrity (#1), she's not a twin (#8), and working for or being any part of the Minnesota Twins does not count.

"How, Flip?" I ask, "how is traveling to Minnesota an accomplishment that will lead to a better life? And do not say happiness, I will slap an asterisk next to your name in a heartbeat."

Flip looked at me as if he had an argument, but just couldn't get it out. From brain to mouth, nothing was going to make this point. He turned to Jonathan as if looking for an ally.

Jonathan threw his arms up, "Hey, you give me shit for my asterisk, if you are going to argue that point you better be prepared to fight for it alone."

"It'll be fun," Flip tries to sell us, "it'll be an adventure. The three of us, the open road. We can end up in New York City on the way back. Who knows what kind of trouble we can get into there."

"I don't want to go to New York Thanksgiving weekend, it's going to be a zoo," I say.

"Ulysses, you've never been there. Besides, the real trip is St. Paul. And if you don't like New York, how about Atlantic City?"

"Um," Jonathan interrupts, "how's that better? At least in New York they clean up after the animals."

"I'm not going to beg you guys, but we all had fun last spring, and I think we all have to rekindle that magic." Flip has a flare for the melodramatic.

Last spring, as with the springs before, the three of us went the Daytona Beach. I went to college in Florida, about one hour north of Daytona. For three years, I told these two they should join me for spring break, but they didn't listen. Both went to school up here close to home. Well, my senior year they smartened up and for four days and three nights we had the time of our lives. Both Flip and I hooked up; however, I'm sure mine was with a woman. Flip was rather drunk, and we found him the next morning in the hallway of our hotel passed out.

He mentioned something about not having on his underwear when he came to in this "girl's" hotel room, but quickly became evasive about the subject. We pushed him a little bit, and he said something about the girl having a twin brother. As the story goes, they were talking in the bedroom, a little kissing, a little more talking, and then the next thing he knows, he passed out. He didn't remember much, but when he woke up, on the other end of the bed was a guy who could have been, according to Flip, her twin brother. Other than his hair being very short, almost shaved, they looked identical. The whole story seemed weird. I'm sure once he sobered up he went right in the shower and checked his butt. He never saw the mystery girl again, though he did run into her brother later that day. He's a handsome man. Flip swears up and down that he got to her room and passed out. He doesn't talk about it much, but thankfully it hasn't prevented him from booking our trip every year. Soon we'll be too old for spring break; hopefully we have one more year in us.

Last year was fun. We went a week after the real peak of the partying, partially because we wanted to golf, partially because we wanted to relax a bit more, but mainly because we just couldn't stay up until three in the morning for five nights. Flip met this girl, Dusty. She was hot. Twenty-one years old, a public-relations major at the University of Florida, from St. Paul, Minnesota. Allegedly she asked him to join her for Thanksgiving. Flip's an only child, his mother died when he was ten, and, soon after, his father ran off, leaving him with his grandparents. They both passed away recently, so this is his second holiday season with no one. Wait; let me correct that, with no family. He's always invited over either my family's or Jonathan's. However, saying that does not invoke a sympathetic response from beautiful twenty-one year old PR majors.

As the story goes, he had her in our hotel room, getting ready to go for her belt when she said stop. He stopped, but started up again real soon. Again she stopped, and they talked all night long. He fell in love, or so he says. They vowed to meet up again, but couldn't figure on a date. Eventually one of them said Thanksgiving. In March, these two make a date for Thanksgiving. What the hell is that?

So now Flip wants to go out there and see her, through hell or high water. But he wants us to go, just in case things don't work out. We have this conversation at least once or twice a week, and I always put the hex on it.

He does not even know her last name.

"Flip," I ask, "when was the last time you spoke with Dusty?"

His response is almost euphoric. "March 28th."

Then Jonathan will jump in. "How do you know where she lives?"

"How many Dustys do you think live in Minnesota and in Gainesville, Florida? There's a little thing called the Internet, where if you have enough time you can get an address."

"So you are just going to surprise her?" I conclude.

"Yeah."

With heads shaking, Jonathan and I walk off; it's time to go to work.

Typically enough, my day ends. I leave

work, get on the train, scout for Ranger-girl, and arrive at my parking lot. I have to drive about two miles to my apartment, a little one bedroom/one bathroom place with a view of a fake lake. The lake is actually a drainage pool, but the ducks don't seem to mind. About a year ago, I lived in a two-bedroom with a female roommate, Bette. No, nothing ever happened. Not only was she not my type, but I found her physically appalling. Call me a pig, call me shallow, but there is something about a dress size greater than my shoe size that I don't care for. She was a good roommate, stayed out of my business, took care of the cable and phone bills, but on occasion she'd bounce her rent check. Boy, would that piss me off. Now my only roommate is Little Jack. He—or maybe he's a she, I'm not 100% sure—but anyway, LJ is my hamster. I've had him for the last two months. Did you know that hamsters are nocturnal, and do all their playing at night? I didn't know that until the first night, more like one in the morning. He started playing in his little hamster wheel. His squeaky little hamster wheel. By that morning, LJ was moved out of my bedroom and into the living room, next to the TV.

Living alone can be fun, but most the time it's really dull. Sure, the excitement of going out on a Friday night, picking up a sexy red head and bringing her home is intoxicating, but in the last year it hasn't happened once. Even if it did happen I'm sure it would be nothing to write home about, not that I'm not really going to write home and tell my mother I picked up a trashy drunk girl at a bar. On weekends I try to make up for the dullness and predictability in my life. My friends come over here because, most notably, my place is clean and I don't have parents or a wife; we can talk bad, watch dirty movies, play video games, all with a healthy dose of beer. However, that's the weekend, and this is Monday.

By six o'clock, my shoes are off, I'm in my boxers—being half-naked is cheaper than AC—and rummaging through my fridge and cabinets looking for food I know isn't there. Looks like another Mac & Cheese night. If there's no baseball on, I'll flip around the channels looking for something, anything to pass the time until I fall asleep. I like to squeeze in a little video game time before bed. My main vices are the sports games, especially football. I like to create myself, and follow my career. I won't necessarily use myself on my team; sometimes I'll let myself get picked up by another team in the game. That way I can follow my career with a sense of pride. I beam when, at the end of a season, I check the Pro Bowl roster and see Ulysses McHugh's name. That's my boy.

What really sucks about living alone is bedtime. When all the lights are off and you're lying in bed, you really start to evaluate life. This is all I have, a bed, a TV, an apartment, a car, a hamster and a job. If I died in my sleep, how long would I lie here before anyone came looking? What's stopping me from packing all my clothes, getting into my car, and starting a life in Maui? Not my job, I can do that crap anywhere. I don't have a girlfriend, though I'd miss Ranger-girl. I'd miss my friends, but...but what? How much would I really miss them? I'd make new friends. I'd make exotic island friends with boats and motorcycles, and leis. We'd drink bright beautiful concoctions out of coconuts. And there would be sun, lot of sun. And the beach. And happiness.

The worst part about sleeping has to be waking up. I love to sleep. When I was in college I was a residence assistant on the freshman hall. I was pretty lenient with those guys, but we had a deal. Wednesday was my day. I would go to sleep at eight PM, and god help them if any one of them woke me up prior to ten AM. These days I'm happy whenever I get six hours of sleep per night during the week. Six hours is never enough for me. You see, I don't really sleep six hours; I close my eyes for six hours. My mind refuses to rest; I dream from the time I hit the pillow to the moment my alarm kicks off.

My dreams are always so incoherent. Yes, there is always the nameless/faceless stock dream character popping up now and then, but often my dreams have celebrities like Bono, Prince Charles, or hundred of M&Ms that regale me in praise as I continuously eat one after another.

What the hell does that mean? Hello, Freud, a little help here. It can't be sexual. Nothing Oedipal here. I once heard that every person in your dream is you, but who the hell was the M&M? As much as I love sleep, I fear sleep. What dreams may come indeed.

My life really hasn't changed much over the past few months, and I really don't see any major difference on the horizon. Sure, I dream about running off to some better place, but really, things aren't that bad. Come 6:30 in the morning, I'm awake. I have seventy minutes to shave, shower, dress, and get to the train. Piece of cake—as a matter of fact, hitting the snooze button is a daily option. I go to work, come home, work, home, work, home, etc. Toss in Ranger-girl on occasion, and that's life. And I'm doing okay with it; I'm relatively prepared for what comes my way. Or so I think.

At work, the crowd is young and we occa-

sionally like to go out and have a couple drinks. With the exception of Jonathan, Dwayne, Kristen and Donna, most of us are single. I'm single because I'm clueless about women in every possible way. Flip, on the other hand, is single because he's an idiot. He'd like you to believe he's single because he's saving himself for Dusty, but really, he's an idiot.

The name of the bar was Make Waves. An outside bar, by the water, just south of town. They had volleyball, basketball, a stage, dancing, and, oh yes, lots of cold beer. The name of the hurricane was Donald. It had ninety mile an hour winds, twenty-foot waves, and oh yeah, the destructive force of an H-bomb. Donald must have had something against Make Waves, because when it was done huffing and puffing, the bar was slightly north of town, and east of town, and downtown. What does this mean to me? Well, Donald hit the last week in September, the same time as North Union's annual end-of-summer party. Due to the storm, the party was moved to a bar closer to work and scheduled two weeks later. Why am I telling you this? Well, because of this change, instead of taking an early train home on the day of the party and driving to Make Waves, I stayed in town and took a later train back home. It's probably a real good thing I took the train, because it helped me sober up. By the time I got to my car, I was okay to drive, but I was emotionally socked. Sometimes when I drink, I think about women. I think about how nice it would be if I had a girlfriend. Someone cuddly I could come home to, who would kiss my lips and call me a corny nickname like sugar foot or something.

I pull out of the train station and there she is: Danger-girl.

I have to fill you in about Danger-girl. Lately on my drive home from the train station, I've been noticing her. There's no way she's older than me, my guess is she's around twenty-two. When I pull out of the train station she's walking down the street, either one way or the other. I figure she lives in one of the tenement buildings nearby, and is walking to a friend's house. I've named her Danger-girl for no real reason other than this really isn't a great neighborhood. I hope she's careful.

Anyway, there she is. It's past eleven at night, why is she walking around? While I'm stopped at the traffic lights by the train station, she stops and looks at me. It's a weird look, as if to say, "Hey, what are you up to? Ever wonder if the right girl might be walking by you repeatedly during the week?" As I drive by her I smile, and she smiles back, kind of winking with a head nod. Could she have possibly been noticing me all this time too? I am a stud.

By the time I get home I'm pretty assured of my lady-killer image. Why I didn't stop for Danger-girl, I don't know. I really wasn't prepared to be hit on at a traffic light by a walker-by. Why don't I prepare for these things?

My alarm is set, and I go to bed. Oh boy, five hours of sleep tonight. Maybe in my dreams tonight I'll have a set of balls.

The day after drinking for me is usually when I'm the most clear-headed. I don't know why, I just feel as if the night before I exorcised demons or something. Unfortunately, North Union's end of summer parties are always Thursday nights (because the company puts money towards the party as a perk, they believe the idea of working the next day will keep the party in check. Not a chance).

It's a slow Friday; Donna has a hicky on her neck. I wonder how that got there. She and Kristen didn't even come to the party. Flip called in sick, some story about being slipped something in his drinks that gave him diarrhea. It could not have been his lunchtime sizzling beef at the Malaysian place we went to yesterday. He is a very paranoid boy. If the government isn't watching his activities for some reason, then they're planning conspiracies to dummy down America, or so Flip believes.

Everyone wants to take off early today: it's a beautiful fall day, who knows how many more we'll have before it turns cold? At four, the exodus starts. Usually I take the 5:16 train home, but today it's the 4:40 if I hurry.

By the time I get to the train station I realize a lot of other people had my idea. I end up having to stand in between the walls because there are absolutely no seats to be had. I'll sacrifice a thirty-minute train ride standing to get home that much earlier. The whistle blows, and moments before the train doors close, Billy Dee Williams jumps on board. He's not really Billy Dee, but he is the spitting image of Lando Calrisian. Strong-looking black guy with his afro jelled back; he's going for the Billy Dee look.

"I really didn't think I'd make it," Billy Dee says to me as if I were waiting for him. There's something familiar about him, beyond the fact he looks just like Billy Dee Williams. "A cab and three trains to get here, and I still had to run." Now I notice the sweat dipping from his forehead, or is that gel? What is so familiar about him, other than the obvious? "I'm just happy I didn't have to take a bus. I freakin' hate the bus, all those drivers are crazy, and you always sittin' next to a freak." What is so familiar about him?

"Yeah, I know what you mean," I said, though I really didn't. I, too,

23

hate taking a bus. The last bus I took was in ninth grade. How am I supposed to know about bus frequenters? The only bus person I knew before this guy was Sandra Bullock.

"Man, I have to run for this train every single day." Mental note: never take the 4:40 again.

BOURBON!

That's what is so familiar about this guy, he stinks of bourbon. Oh my god, why weren't my headphones on when I first got on the train?

Like an idiot who can't be rude and shrug someone off, I begin to have a conversation with this fellow. "Well, at least it's not too hot out, today was really nice."

"Oh man, I like the heat, as a matter of fact, in a month or two I'm moving to Vegas."

I've always wanted to go there. "Vegas huh, that's great." Shit, I'm in a conversation.

"Man, I just came back, oh what a town." Suddenly this man's eyes light up, and I have the sneaky suspicion I'm about to hear about his Vegas trip. "Every day ninety degrees, every building air conditioned, every casino has free drinks and wicked cheap buffets. Did you know you can get a lobster for eight bucks a pound? Shit. Oh, and the women. Mmmm, mmmmm! Only beautiful women out there and you can have them all."

No, he did not just say that. Oh, God help me, now I'm scared.

"When I got off the plane, a limo picked me up and took me on a tour of the strip. When the driver dropped me off he gave me a card, on the card was a phone number. He said that after I'm settled in my room to call and within fifteen minutes a beautiful woman will be there."

"Wow," I can't believe this. Maybe I'll get off before my stop today. This can't be happening. Should I ask him about Siegfried and Roy? That'll change the subject. "Did you see any shows?"

"Oh yeah. After this one show I went to this club, and around four in the morning, when some of the waitresses got off, they invited everyone back to their house. All free. Booze and women. That was a good time, and everyone is like that. You're always invited back to parties, and it's all free."

"Wow." This guy is a piece of work.

"Oh, and they got that Mustang Ranch out there," he says.

Please God, no, please.

"The women there are incredible. They have pictures of all the ladies and you just pick the one you want. You go to a room, and that girl shows up fifteen minutes later."

So the hookers run on a fifteen minute schedule...I wonder what the bus schedule is like?

"And if you don't like her, send her back and another will come up. Oh man, nothing better."

Humoring him, I say that it's all hard to imagine, but Billy Dee just retells his tales to solidify to me that yes, it's all true. Either he recognizes that I look like the type of guy someone can talk to out of the blue, or he works for the Vegas Chamber of Commerce, and he's spotted me as a good "John" prospect. The train stops.

"Man," Billy Dee says reaching out his hand, "it was nice talking to you, have a good one."

"You too my friend, stay cool." And like that, it was over. "I have to put on my headphones immediately every time I get on this train." A small Asian woman looks up at me, and I smile.

As interesting as that train ride was, it revealed one thing to me. Sex is out there, and I'm not having any of it. Okay, going three thousand miles just to find a hooker might be a little too much, but why can't I just pick up a good-looking woman, take her home, and hook up, preferably without paying for it in the morning. I'm a good-looking guy, I can just go into a bar, and I'm bound to attract someone. By this time, I'm in my car heading home. That's when I see her. It's Danger-girl, and she's walking the same direction I'm driving and we've recently exchanged glances. "Gosh, how do I do this, should I just pull over and introduce myself? Maybe I should just drive on, and forget this. It's crazy." And then, fate lends a hand, or rather a thumb. Her thumb pops up. She needs a ride. Is this what fate is? Quickly, I pull over.

"Hey, do you need a ride?" I say, very mature and suave. I figure she's a street-smart girl with a lot of common sense. All she needs is a break. I'm a successful banker. I could be that break. We could do a lot for each other. This could be that start you only hear about in the movies.

"I'm glad you stopped," she said smiling as she jumped in my car. "I've spotted you a couple times, but figured you weren't interested."

Wow, she moved fast. Nothing subtle about her. "Oh, I've been interested, but I was a little nervous to meet you like this. I'm Ulysses." I start to pull away from the curb, and drive down the road.

"I'm Alice, what do you have in mind?"

She moves real fast. I figured some small talk, then I ask her out, but she must have been doing a bit of planning. What a great girl. "Where do you want me to drive you to?"

"Take this right, are you looking for a date?"

Am I, it's been a while. I need a date. Boy, is she fast. "Yeah, are you hungry? Want to get a pizza?"

"Cute. You're not a cop, are you?"

Odd question. "Why?"

"You sound like a cop. Are you a cop?"

This time, as she asks the question, she starts to frisk me, in rather personal places. "Whoa. Hey. What are you doing?"

"Do you want a date or what? I don't have time to play around. It's thirty bucks for a blow job and seventy-five for sex, but you can't cum inside me. I don't have any rubbers, but if you do, that's cool, but you still can't cum inside me."

Oh my God. "Oh my God, I…um…you're a…I think I made a mistake." I can't believe this. Am I that stupid? I picked up a hooker, in broad daylight, during commuter hours, at the train station I go to every day.

She jumps in during my silence, "You know, why don't you take me back to where you picked me up?"

I quickly turn around, and back we go. "I'm sorry," I say staring straight towards the road ahead.

She snaps, "Sorry doesn't get me and my son food, thanks for nothing."

As I get to our original location, I try to make amends. "Here, take it," I pull out five bucks from my shirt pocket. "What is that, fucking charity?" She picks it out of my hand, jumps out of my car, and slams the door. As I drive off, I look into the rearview mirror, and there she is, already over our indiscretion, thumbing down another car.

For months, at least three, I've seen her. Let's say she sees four guys a day, four times thirty days in a month is 120. That's 360 in the last three months. At thirty bucks a pop, she's made $9000. Throw in a couple big-ticket items at $75 a shot, and she's probably made over ten grand in the last three months. That's forty grand a year. Shit, that's what I make, but I bet she doesn't pay taxes. She's had relations with all those men, and there she was, sitting in my car. I'm going to be sick.

I reach this epiphany at the same time I reach my apartment. I wonder how many people saw her get in my car. If each car on the train holds one hundred people, and there are ten cars, then 1000 people were on my train as it left. I'm the third stop of seven, which average about 150 people per stop. If that many got off at my stop, and half of them went in my direction, that means 75 people, who live in this city with me, who work in the same city I work, and who take the same train I took, saw me casually pick up a prostitute. I'm home now, and I realize I hate doing math in my head almost as much as I hate throwing up on my shoes, and I just threw up on my shoes.

"Are you all right?" asks an old woman who lives in my apartment complex.

"Just fine." I swing open my door, kick off my shoes, and head for the bathroom. I throw up again. There's no way in hell I'm going outside my apartment ever again.

With my stomach calmed down, I try to

sleep. I think about a lot of things: my life, my trouble with women, my job and friends and family. Nothing seemed to make sense, nothing except the desire to sleep. I stay in my apartment all weekend, avoiding the phone. I go to bed early on Sunday, hoping more rest would get me ready for work. At midnight, I decide to call in sick, I really feel like I did something wrong, but I know I didn't. Why can't I escape these feelings?

If I thought that what I experienced after work that day was scary, what I faced that night was worse. My typical sleep is laced with incoherent dreams screaming volumes, but saying nothing. Tonight something that never happened before challenged my sleep. In the midst of my third dream of the night involving Alice, the one where we were walking on my parents' kitchen appliances, trying to avoid the squirrels that roamed the floor, I suddenly awoke. Normally, my dreams have a beginning, middle, and definitive end; however, this time I jerked out of bed suddenly and violently. There was some street light bleeding in through the window, and it was just enough to shed light on the most amazing thing I ever saw. Hovering not three feet above me, with an expression as shocked on its face as I'm sure I had on mine, was a small, maybe two foot tall pink elephant. Not just any small, pink elephant, but one wearing lederhosen. I blinked and rubbed my eyes, not sure if I was really awake or still sleeping. As my eyes get clear, the image kept fading further away. I struggled to focus and as my eyes finally became right, it was gone.

I shook my head and tried desperately to comprehend what I saw. I really could not tell if I was sleeping or awake. 5:16 am. Way too early to focus my eyes, let alone my brain. For that moment I forgot about Alice, but as consciousness started to overcome me, my earlier indiscretion resurfaced. I threw some water on my face and went back to bed. I stared at my ceiling for about an hour until I fell back asleep.

My forth dream about Alice that night started in my car. Basically it followed the same path as our actual encounter, but when I asked her if she wanted a pizza, she said yes, and we suddenly were in a park, eating a pizza pie. After she ate a slice, she told me it'll cost thirty dollars for a slice, and seventy-five for the entire thing. I was furious, absolutely engulfed by rage. I lashed out at her, but as I grabbed her head I realized she was actually Ranger-girl. Ring... Ring. The phone woke me. "Hello."

"Does someone have a tummy-ache? Do you want some coffee ice cream?"

It's nice to know you can always rely on your friends to pick you up when you are down, and try to make you feel worse than you actually are. "Hi, Jonathan."

"Hey, I have Flip with me, where are you?"

"I just don't feel like myself, I kind of had a tough weekend."

Flip jumped in. "What was her name, stud?"

"I'm not in the mood, man, what do you guys need?"

"Hey," Jonathan jumped in, "we're just calling to see if you're all right. Are you sick? We just haven't heard from you all weekend."

Before I could answer, Flip interjected. "Dude, you should call for a nurse to come and give you a sponge bath. I think they got that shit in the yellow pages."

Instead of arguing, I just went along with him. "Good idea, I'll tell you how it goes. I'm going back to bed. I'll talk to you later." I hung up the phone before they could stop me. It's 10:24, still a lot of sleeping I have to do before I feel better.

No sooner did I hit the pillows then the phone rang again. "What?"

"Man, it's me, Flip. Quick question."

"What?"

He starts pleading. "Thanksgiving is, like, six weeks away. Jonathan will go if you go, but only if you go. Five days of your life, I promise it will be totally worth it."

I snap. "Yeah, for you. Not to be an asshole, man, but why should I? Would you ever sacrifice five days of your life for me? Have you ever sacrificed five of anything for anyone but yourself?"

"Um... no." There was a silence. "Sorry, I'll let you get back to sleep." In that brief exchange, Flip went from excited to dejected. Good job, Ulysses.

I have to take a piss. As much as I want to stay and sleep, I have to pee. I'm not yet at the stage of urinating on myself, but I can't imagine it being too far away. I'm sure LJ would like something to eat; just because I'm an idiot, he doesn't have to suffer.

I shake the hamster food container to see if I can get a reaction. He's not a dog; what am I looking for? LJ can be pretty funny when you first wake him up. He's groggy, so you can grab him, then he realizes he's out of his cage and frantically runs, but all I do is roll my hands one in front of the other, and he goes nowhere. After a minute, he settles down and I can put him in my shirt pocket for a while. He doesn't hate it, but I think he gets a little nervous—sometimes I'll find little hamster poop inside my pocket. It's not as bad as it sounds.

"LJ, front and center… oh shit." The pipe that leads from the main cage to a smaller side cage is separated from its fitting. LJ is free. Frantically, I check around the apartment, under the couch, between the cushions, behind the TV. He's nowhere. Hell, I don't even remember seeing him last night, I was in bed for nearly two days. He could be anywhere. He could have gotten out. He could be stuck in the wall. He could be bullied by mice or squirrels, or an owl might have swept down to the ground and picked him up, so now he's dead in a tree somewhere. "Shit!!!"

Not only am I a "John" now, but my hamster's lost somewhere and probably dead. This sucks. "Lucky rock, my ass!" I reach into my right pocket to pull out my rock, and it's not there. I have not been without this rock in my pocket for two years. Now it's missing and life sucks. "Shit!" I head to my bedroom, slam the door, and bury my head in a pillow. Maybe I'll wake up from this shitty dream, or maybe I'll just suffocate under this pillow. Either way, everything right now sucks big time.

By 7:25 pm the next night, I'm awake, showered, and feeling a little better. I really miss Little Jack, I hope he's okay. I still have not given up hope that he's alive, so this afternoon I dropped some food in the middle of the living room. Either the pile will decrease because of him, or the next owner of the apartment better have a vacuum. I'm hungry; I really haven't had anything to eat in almost four days. Isn't self-pity grand? Will it be a macaroni and cheese night, or ravioli night? Just as I decide on ravioli, Jonathan comes knocking on the door.

"Hey, how are you doing?"

"Better."

"Good, get your clothes on, we're getting drunk."

"I don't know, Jonathan."

"Get your clothes on, we are drinking. No ifs, ands, or buts, hear me." He sounds determined.

"Someone once said IF is in the middle of LIFE." That's enough for me right now. I grab my house keys, and my jacket. As we walk out to the parking lot, what do I find in my right jacket pocket? My rock. A smile crosses my face as I reload the rock from jacket pocket to the right pant pocket. I'm starting to feel better.

Minutes later, we are at a pub down the street, The Snow House, making a bee-line straight for the corner of the bar. The corner is prime real estate, especially when there are just two of you. No awkward bends and turns to talk. You can scan one region of the bar while your friend scans another. There are few, if any, downsides to the corner.

Jonathan starts, "You want to talk about it?"

"Not yet."

The Celtics are on, pre-season versus the Mavericks, and for a few awkward moments we both stare at the TV, waiting for the bartender. A Sam Adams and a Rolling Rock. "Well, if you're not talking, I will," says Jonathan. "Round two. Dany's pregnant again, about six weeks. We just found out yesterday. I was going to take you guys to lunch, but you've been bagging us at work."

Perspective. Suddenly, I feel like a huge jerk. I put down my Rolling Rock and hug Jonathan. These last few days feel really trivial in light of Jonathan's good news. "Congratulations. How's Dany?"

"Oh, she's great; a little worried, but great. You know, she didn't tell me for three days. When she did, we both cried for an hour. It was the happiest cry of my life." Jonathan was beaming as he tilted back his Sam Adams. "Which brings me to my point; I think we should go to Minnesota with Romeo. I can't go to Florida next year, Dany will be too far along, knock on wood." Jonathan actually knocks on his head. "I can't take that chance."

After a quick moment and a long gulp of Rolling Rock I look at Jonathan and start to laugh. "How is it your pregnant wife is allowing you to go on such a fool's errand over Thanksgiving?"

Jonathan raises his hand and motions for another round. "It's our year. You had Flip last year, this is our year. Dany is well-aware this is our year to take Flip in. Between you and me, she's not a big fan of Flip, but she knows how close we are and could never say no. This way, I see Flip and spend Thanksgiving with him and she doesn't have to. Win–win."

Obviously Dany does not mind that I am saddled with Flip three years in a row, with, I have the feeling, many more to come. I'll have to find a reason to skip Thanksgiving next year and pass Flip back. Maybe I'll meet a Native American girl and tell everyone that Thanksgiving insults her people. Maybe I'll stop worrying about that and try to date any girl by next year.

At this point I just give in. After all, how bad could it be? "You got it. Besides, it'll be a cheap trip; lover boy is paying our way. Besides, who really wants to play golf in Florida in April anyway?"

There's a roar from the TV—the Celtics just scored. It seems this is one of the happiest moments in a long while for a lot of people. We sit and watch the game, and by half-time Flip shows up.

"Is it safe?" He has a way of defusing me.

"I don't know, do I have to bring these people a gift if we barge in unannounced on Thanksgiving?"

His face lights up. I'm with the two happiest people in the world. I order a round of shots, and the three of us discuss our immediate future plans. The Celtics have a six-point lead to start the second half; things are turning out ok.

With twenty seconds left, the Celtics had a three point lead on the Mavs and the ball. A turnover with seven seconds, and a three-pointer by some white guy who looks like he just graduated Cornbread State in Indiana, and it's tied with no time on the clock. And he was fouled. Swish, the free throw is good, and the Celts grab defeat from victory. It'll be a long season. Go Bruins. After a tough overtime loss, the men in green walk off the floor dejected; they're probably cheering for the Bruins too. With that, the three of us take the cue and walk out of the Snow House. We have to go to work tomorrow. I walk Jonathan to his car and congratulate him again. "I have a good feeling about this." He smiles, a bit choked-up, shakes my hand. "Hey, is the party still on, or does this change everything?"

"It's still on; I told her we should wait to tell our parents. I suggested we get both sets over for dinner, but I think we'll do it at the party." Jonathan answered. "But as of now, it's still a surprise."

I asked Jonathan if she has any clue about the party. "None at all and aside from you two, no one has any idea she's pregnant. Bring tissues." We shake hands and I walk to my car.

Frank Hughes, Jr.

I spend the first two minutes in my car finding a radio station. It's either the Celtics' post-game show, or music. The Celtics lost, so music it is. I dig out my Stone Temple Pilots CD, and I'm off. The Snow House is down the road from my little place; if it was a better neighborhood I'd walk, but not here.

I'm not a block from the pub, and there she is, Alice, hitch-hiking. I'm in a line of five cars passing by her. The first two drive on, the guy in front of me checks her out, but he doesn't look long since he has a passenger. I can't blame him; she is looking really hot tonight: a tight little half-shirt, with a jacket wrapped around her small, thin waist, covering her perfect, round butt. She's wearing a baseball cap backwards, a Red Sox cap; at least she supports the home team. The only drawback, aside from her being a hooker, is the footwear. She has flip-flops on. It's fall, and she's wearing flip-flops. I hate flip-flops, that stupid thip-thop…thip-thop, why aren't they called thip-thops? And the sound just sends a shiver up my spine. I bet her toes are wicked dirty. They have to be, walking outside with nothing but flip-flops between you and nature. I look at my car floor and wonder what she was wearing when I had her in my beautiful Mustang. I'll vacuum after work tomorrow night.

As I drive by we make eye contact, but there is no acknowledgement from her. Does she see me as absolutely no potential income, and therefore ignores my presence, or am I simply not in the correct location within the parade of cars to seriously contend for her rented affection? No sooner do I think that when car number five (actually a minivan) pulls over, and I can see her jump in through my rearview mirror. I feel bad for her. I feel bad for him. He obviously has a family; he's driving a minivan, a green minivan, probably picked out by his wife. I stop at the red light on Main and Simpson, still watching the drama behind me. Maybe I'm wrong. Maybe she was actually going home; it is late, and maybe she knows the guy in the minivan. Green light. I line up to take a left, but I have to wait for oncoming traffic. The minivan approaches, and at the light, takes a right down Simpson Street. I think for a second and ask myself, why would she be hitch-hiking on one street, and why would her driver take her down another? There is no more oncoming traffic. Wouldn't Alice hitch-hike on the street that she wants to travel on? As the light turns yellow, I drive straight. One quick test, if I can get a block ahead, and track where Alice and "John" are going, I'll find out if this is a personal trip, or professional. What I do after that, I have no idea.

I'm going way too fast for this neighborhood. I get to the corner of Ogilbee and Airth and watch. There's a red light at Simpson and Airth; if I'm lucky, they are caught at the light. Sure enough, a green minivan takes a right onto Airth. That's a 180 degree turnabout from her original direction. The pursuit is on. I turn right onto Airth and follow discreetly. They pass Sica Drive and take a left on Dutson. I take a left on Sica and gun it. At the corner of Sica and First Avenue, I wait. There is no way they got to First Avenue before me. No way. Knowing a little about this part of town, I really don't want to sit on Sica and First, so I go hunting. I take a right, then another right down Dutson and wouldn't you know, there's a green minivan. But something is odd; the minivan is parked in front of a house, with a porch light on. Maybe I was wrong, maybe Alice lives there, or maybe the guy driving lived there. Maybe they are friends, and he was helping her out. Maybe I think too much. I sneak a peak at the minivan as I drive by, and there's nothing exciting to report. By the time I get to the end of the street I'm confident in the fact that I think too much. Yet, there was something about that minivan. Something elusive. At the lights on Airth and Simpson it hits me. A quick swipe up with my left hand, and I go left: home. To right: the unknown.

I follow my previous track and head down Dutson, and as I get closer to the minivan it hits me, there's no seat on the driver's side of the car. I can clearly see the passenger's seat, but the driver's seat is not there. I'm traveling at about 10 mph and just as I'm about to pass, my suspicion is proven right. I see Alice's ass rise from the reclined driver's seat and lower. Say what you will about her chosen profession, it doesn't deny the fact that she has a wonderful ass.

For some strange reason, I feel monumentally better. In addition to Jonathan's good news, and Flip's elation over our trip, I catch a regular family guy jeopardizing his life, family, job and future for a thirty-dollar blow job. That's sad. That's pathetic. What I fell into was a mistake I quickly remedied; this guy certainly didn't pick her up by mistake and say, "Oops, my pants fell down," at the same time she collapsed into his lap.

This guy was probably watching the same game I was at home, the kids in bed, his wife doing the bills. He probably told her he was going

out for cigarettes, or to pick up the kids' ear medicine. A quick five, ten minute detour and he's done. Time to complete the cover story, and head home. Maybe he opted for the condom, maybe not. Either way, the chance of him infecting his wife with an STD is greatly enhanced. Before any symptoms pop up, he'll probably have sex with her. Even in a bad marriage, people have urges. He infects her, now suddenly both parents are diagnosed with an incurable STD. Maybe she stays with him, maybe she doesn't; either way, they are both dead in 15 years. Now their toddler is a teenage orphan with no one to care for her, and she turns to drugs to get through the day. Soon the inheritance runs out and she has a hundred-dollar-a-day crack habit. Before long she turns to the streets, and prostitution, and she's in minivans offering whatever she can for a few bucks. That's really sad.

Just as I'm next to the minivan, I start flashing my high beams and honking my horn. As they both look up, I smile out the window and speed off. Maybe not the smartest thing I've ever done, considering Alice knows where I park my car, but it was fun to see them jump up. As I turned off Dutson, I saw the car lights of the minivan turn on behind me. I guess I ruined someone's night.

I pull into my parking space with a smile. What a night, I don't think I've ever experienced anything quite like this. One thing is for sure, I haven't smiled this much in a couple of days.

As I open the door to my apartment

I'm very careful to watch my step, fearing to crunch my rogue hamster, if indeed he has not yet escaped the confines of my apartment. I turn on the light, and I'm immediately drawn to the center of the living room floor. Sitting in the middle of the pile of food, looking up at me with those big, round black eyes in absolute shock is Little Jack. He's alive! "LJ, where have you been?" Do I expect an answer? No sooner are the words out of my mouth, the taste of freedom is escaping Little Jack. With pouches full of fresh food, he darts for the bathroom.

Now I'm not so smug as to think I can easily capture a twelve-ounce hamster, but the hunt is on. I run into the bathroom and corner LJ behind the toilet. Oh man, this is disgusting, I really should clean behind here. My plan is simple— I'll fake to the right, flush him out, then come back to the left and grab my escapee. Sure enough, one lunge right, LJ is going left. I can outsmart a hamster. I follow him as he runs under the bathroom vanity. He's going nowhere; I'll just corner him off, and pick him up.

As LJ gets to the end of the line, I see his little body stretch and climb up a small hole under the cabinet. "Shit." I grab his back legs, and start to pull. For a little hamster, he's got a good grip on whatever it is he's using to climb. I become very aware that my grip might be a little too firm. I don't want to hurt LJ. "Shit!" I release my grip, and let him go. He's alive, and I'm happy, but in all honesty, I'm less than impressed by the fact that I was just outmanuvered by a hamster on the run. Well, it's a long night, Little Jack; let's see where we end up in the morning.

I need supplies. A flash light, a shoebox, and Tupperware. The Tupperware goes on the bathroom counter. The shoebox stays with me, the flashlight sits in my back pocket. I decide to increase the portion of food in the center of the living room to maybe entice my prey. I need a high perch to watch from, close, yet out of sight. The bathroom counter. I'll wait on top of the bathroom counter, and then when LJ gets greedy and goes for more food, I'll spring my trap. Now all there is left to do is wait.

Forty minutes later, I hear a small rustling, like so many little fingers stuffing food into a cheek pouch. "The game is afoot." I hope my landlord is not secretly videotaping my apartment. I reach down, under the bathroom vanity, and block the spot with the hole using the shoebox. Escape route cut off. Next I slowly walk through the bathroom into my bedroom so I can get in front of LJ and once again force him into the bathroom. Slowly I open my bedroom door, step through, and close it. It's very dark in the apartment, and either LJ doesn't see me, or he doesn't see me as a threat. That'll soon change. I take the flash light out of my pocket, aim to the noise of hamster hoarding, and bam, lights on. Oh, did that take him by surprise, he did not count on the element of light. After a stunned moment, LJ assesses his situation and runs for the bathroom again. From behind the toilet I think he thinks he can fake me out again. Before I make my move, I grab the Tupperware bowl in the sink.

"It's either you or me, buddy." I lunge right, he runs left until—oh, somebody put a shoebox where the escape hole was. I take this moment to trap my prey before he can figure out his own plan B. Thwap. I bring the Tupperware down, and trap my elusive foe. Oh, I feel the weight off my shoulders now. I feel like things have turned around 180 degrees from Monday. "Thank God," I reach in my pocket and grab my rock, "never disappear again," I say to the rock, then I look down at LJ, "and you, well, I hope we had fun the last few days, 'cause it's cage time now, baby."

I don't immediately go to bed, even though

it's midnight, I'm not very tired. I figure I can sit in my chair, turn on the TV, close my eyes, think about life, and gradually fall asleep. Sometime around two in the morning, I'll wake up and drag myself to bed. I'll just sit here, think about LJ's adventure and how much fun he must have had, and let the TV lull me to sleep. Just lull me to sleep. RING!

Oh, that is an awful sensation. With all the technology we have today, why we need a phone that rings is beyond me. RING!

Why not a phone with a soft voice that judges the light in a room and grows softer in low light, simply saying "Telephone call…telephone call," in a nice, female British voice? RING!

I don't want to get up; it's after midnight, and I have an answering machine. I'll definitely screen this one, beside, what inconsiderate asshole calls after midnight? RING!

My answering machine picks up: "Hi, if you don't know what to do now, how did you ever muster the intelligence to dial this number?" Beep.

"Ulysses?" the voice slams over the speaker like a sledge hammer to my ear. It couldn't be, not after six months. The voice continues, "Ulysses, it's Janice, it's been a while, and I came across your number and, well, call me if you want." Before she can finish I'm off the chair, and the phone is in my hand.

"Janice."

"Ulysses."

There is a real odd silence; in reality it lasted three seconds, but it seems at least three hours. Little Jack is staring at me; I can't tell if it is disapproval of Janice, or if he is still in shock that I outsmarted him.

She started. "Hi, sorry I'm calling so late, but I just wanted to say hi." Back six months ago, Janice and I were dating for the third time. All three times, things ended on her terms. First time was over an ex-boyfriend, understandable enough. They went out for two years, and even lived together. We started dating soon after the breakup, and only dated for three months. It takes time to get over someone. The second

39

time was over stress from work and family. Apparently she couldn't balance working Friday nights and Saturday days at the mall as the assistant manager of Sunglass Hut, going to her parents' weekend summer cookouts on Cape Cod, and dating me. Something had to give—guess which? Me. The third time ended because she was feeling pressure from me over getting married. That would be understandable if I ever proposed, but that would involve a ring, and most importantly, a proposal. She's a nut, and she's dumped me three times. That's two times more than any other woman. And now she's setting up number four. I might not be the brightest guy in the world, but if I'm smart enough to find and catch a rouge hamster, then I'm smart enough not to get dumped by the same person four times.

"Yeah, hi," I say coldly, a little cocky.

"So how have you been?" She's trying for conversation.

"Yeah, ok." As if she cares.

"Oh, well, I'll let you go; I caught you at a bad time, take care." She clearly sensed my lack of enthusiasm, and sounded oh so dejected.

"Yeah, bye," I replied.

Click, and she's gone. Janice smoked the entire time we dated, with the exception of a total of three weeks spread over three years of dating, not dating, being friends, dating, not dating, being nothing to each other, being friends, dating, and not dating. I hope she's smoking right now. I hope she's smoking a big, fat, tar-laden, nicotine-filled flaming cancer stick that rips ten years from her life per puff. Maybe that's too rough, maybe five years a puff.

I sit in my chair. She did sound kind of down. Hopefully she just got dumped. Too bad, she deserves some misery. I don't want to call her back. I want her to feel alone and friendless. Why should it be my responsibility to cheer her up? How dare she call me just because she's down and expects me to talk her through whatever is wrong? I wonder what's wrong? She sounded sad. She sucks. Shit, I can't believe I'm going to call her.

Two rings and she answers, clearly she was waiting for her caller ID to kick in; who else would call so late? "Hi," she answers.

"What's wrong, you're only calling me if something's wrong, what's wrong?" I say rather matter-of-factly. I'm pissed, but I called her back. I'm so stupid.

Timidly she speaks. "I've had a really bad couple of days, and I had no one who I could really talk to, and I know you'd understand...." I cut her off.

"...understand because I've gone through tough days also, and you have first hand knowledge of this as both participant and instigator." Good dig. Besides, I've had a bad couple of days also, and I did the right thing, shutting out people, not bothering them after midnight.

"Maybe this was a bad idea," she says.

In my head I agree, but I'm such a pussy when it comes to her. "No, I'm sorry, that's past. What's wrong?"

Janice goes on to tell me that she was passed over for a promotion at work, and that her boss tried to make a move on her. He told her that maybe the next promotion will be hers, however in the meantime she can work on a raise. I chuckle to myself, partially happy someone made her feel like dirt, but continue to offer a sympathetic ear. Soon after that, I invite her over to talk. So stupid.

Morning. Twenty-four hours ago I woke up feeling drained and scared. Too afraid of my own shadow to even walk outside and go to work. Since then, Jonathan is beaming with pride, Flip is excited about Thanksgiving like no other year, Dany's pregnant, Alice is at least thirty bucks richer, the minivan guy went through a bout of frustration, LJ is home, and I got laid. Yes, that's what I said, I got laid, and fortunately, or perhaps unfortunately, it wasn't a prostitute or a sponge bath nurse found in the yellow pages that sent me a sure thing after Janice left, it was with Janice. I am so stupid. Sometime around 2:30 in the morning I told Janice it was late, and I had to work in the morning. We hugged, then we kissed, then ka-boom. So stupid! Not to mention, she's still here. One question keeps ringing in my head, "Is this right?" Don't get me wrong, it was good sex, most times unexpected sex is good sex. She can do this thing with her lips that drives me crazy. She bites my bottom lip, pulls it towards her, and sucks. Oh, that's my sexual Achilles heel, once she does that it's over. I'm awake, but I haven't rolled over yet to look at her. As great as the sex was, why do I open myself up to this? So very stupid.

But there she is, and she's beautiful. Her red hair lies on the pillow, flowing around her. She's so peaceful, so unlike last night when she was crying and sad. Without warning, my alarm goes off. I leap up, and smack the snooze, hoping not to wake her, but it's too late.

"Twenty-four hours ago, this would be the last thing I'd expect," she said in a rough, morning voice with her eyes half-open, reaching over to me. Morning breath is bad enough, but she smoked several cigarettes last night and the smoke seems to be sitting in her mouth, waiting to greet me.

"It's been eventful," I say smiling. I always set my alarm allowing enough time to shit (when applicable), shower, shave, dress, and get to the train. It's really an artful dance I perform every morning. If one element is off, I could miss my train. I do have a built in time saver—sometimes I don't bother shaving—but everything else is a must. This morning I don't have time for small talk with Janice. I haven't shaved for five days, so I leap out of bed, and I'm off to the bathroom. No snooze button this morning.

Two-thirds of my face is covered in shaving cream when Janice enters. "You're in here pretty fast."

"I've got to get ready for work." I slap the last remaining bare spot on my face and turn into the mirror. I think I just hurt her feelings, and in the mirror I see her head drop as she walks away. I've only had two hours of sleep and she wants me to be sweet. "Janice, I have to get ready for work, but I'll call you tonight, I promise." She manages a smile, and gathers her things as I jump in the shower. Somewhere between anxiety and enthusiasm, there's stupidity.

Janice yells goodbye, I dress for work, and by 7:10 I'm on my way out. I do not even notice if Ranger-girl is at the train station today.

For the first time in months, the morning was not dominated with talk of Minnesota. Actually there was little conversation. Jonathan and Flip figured we discussed everything there was to talk about last night, until I dropped my bombshell. "So, I had sex with Janice last night." I said it neither bragging nor guilt ridden, rather informational.

An appropriate reaction follows, and after I fill them in on the phone call, then the conversation, then the kiss, etc., their reaction is swift and decisive.

"Are you stupid?" Flip is first. "I mean come on. Don't you remember Janice? Play by my rules, I'm so wonderful, Janice. I'm so smart, I'm so pretty, Janice. Ulysses, let me build you up and then dump you for no reason at all, Janice."

"Okay, okay. So I've made this mistake before, but not this time. It was just sex. Not a date, no money or emotion involved. Just sex." I countered.

"Yeah, ah-huh, sure. Just sex." Jonathan was quick and to the point. "And when you go out it'll be just as friends. No emotional attachment, right?"

They have me against the ropes, but I battle back. "Listen, I have no desire to date her again. I'll do her, I'll be done by her, and we can hang out, but I'm not going to date her. Give me a little credit, do you really think I'm going to subject myself to going through that crap again?"

Flip just shakes his head and Jonathan continues, "Man, we are just looking out for you. We don't want to see you get hurt."

"Actually," Flip jumps in, "I like it when you get dumped because you usually take us out for drinks, and you end up paying. Hell, thanks to her I've gotten drunk four times, for free."

"Three times," I say.

"Give it a month," Flip replies.

I really don't want to date her, and it's true I will hang out and be a friend, and if I get laid every now and then, who am I to complain? Flip and Jonathan acknowledge my weak plan, and shrug the whole thing off until I drop number two. "I was going to invite her to your anniversary party."

Flip's jaw drops. "Man, that's a date. That is so a date. Anytime you dress up and take a girl to a party with a family you are on a date."

"It's not my family," I counter.

"Doesn't matter, it's still someone's family." Oh, he's mad. "Not only is it a date, but that's a serious date. Now I'm a fifth wheel because my girl is in Minnesota. That sucks. Jonathan, don't let him."

"Thanks for putting me in the middle, Flip," Jonathan pipes in and turns to me, "I told you to bring tissues, not issues. But you're over twenty-one, I can't tell you what to do anymore. Have you already asked her?"

"Yeah, she seemed excited." I wasn't going to ask her, but I hate going to parties solo, and when they are parties of this caliber I feel obligated to bring a date. One of the subjects we talked about last night was Jonathan and Dany, the party came up, and I invited her. If I thought for a second it was inappropriate, I never would have invited her, but I think it'll be harmless enough.

Flip picks his head up as if something profound will come out, maybe he'll be okay with this. "Did you ever wonder why they put the caps lock key so close to the letter "a"? It's a way to dummy down corporate America." From nowhere, Flip delivers this insight, choosing to ignore our previous line of conversation, but thankfully taking the heat off me.

"What?" Jonathan acts puzzled.

Flip had an audience and I'm not too upset that the focus has changed. I really didn't want to talk about Janice anyway. "Have you ever thought about why they put "a" next to the caps lock key? Why put a letter that is used in language 11 % of the time next to a key that not only feeds the laziness, *and* is rather unnecessary. Oh, it's *so* difficult to hold shift, especially when there are two on either end of the keyboard. Think of it, how many times are you typing an important memo, you look up, and the last two lines have been all the wrong case? Then you have to go back, re-write, productivity is lost. And if you don't catch it, you look like an idiot to the recipient."

Where his mind comes up with this stuff, we will never know; how does he know "a" is used 11% of the time? I'll say this, he's entertaining for sure. I ask, "Flip, when you say that "a" is used 11% of the time, I'm assuming in all literature and language. Why not put the caps lock by the "I", surely that's used just as much, if not more."

"You might think that, but doesn't a capital "I" remind you of a lower-case "l" and the number "1"? When you get back to your desk, check it out." Obviously, he's put a lot of thought towards this. "And

44

they plop the "e" just under the "3". Is that the best place for an "e"? What does a capital "e" look like backwards? E... 3... E... 3?" Flip extends three fingers on his right hand and pivots them back and forth, first and "E", then a "3".

"Yeah, and I always get screwed up with the zero and the "o" so close." Jonathan adds fuel to the fire.

"It's all meant to make people look dumber than they are, and keep them in their menial jobs." Flip is full of pride.

"How does misspelling in a memo prevent me from career opportunities?" I inquire.

Flip quickly answers, "No one will take you seriously if you are an idiot." On that line, both Jonathan and I walk away from Flip, recognizing that, by his own words, we should not be taking him serious. Time for us to go back to work and at least pretend to get something done.

After lunch I get an e-mail from half of my favorite duo. Lately I've been their best friend. I'm the only one mature enough to understand how difficult office life is for them. It is a short e-mail:

Ulysses,

Donna and I were wondering if it was alright if we work an occasional SaturdAY SO i CAN HELP TRIAN HER. tHANKS, kRISTEN.

Maybe Flip has something here.

I get her on the phone. "Hi Kristen, work all the Saturdays you want."

"Thanks Ulysses, but those two old jerks downstairs wouldn't let us in this weekend because we didn't have clearance. We came all the way in here and had to go back. I hate those guys, what's the big deal."

Vaguely I recall a memo going to managers that anyone working weekends had to be cleared through security, and they needed a letter from their managers. "Gee Kristen, that's new to me. Let me look into it, and I'll get back to you." Why should I jump through hoops for these two? Sure, eventually I'll fold and write a letter to Clint, but not right now. Actually, I kind of like the notion of Clint and Charles pissing these two off. "Oh, check the cap-lock on your keyboard, I think you hit it accidentally."

"Huh? Oh, it's on. Thanks, Ulysses. Gee, I guess I look pretty stupid."

"No," I assure her, "not at all."

The first thing I notice when I get home is a note

tacked to my door. Did I not pay the rent, did I park in someone's spot, who would leave me a note? In the land of e-mail and voice-mail I get an antiquated tacked-mail. Obviously someone could not afford a stamp. Heck, it's not even in an envelope, it is just folded in thirds. And what is with tacking a letter on my door frame? That leaves a mark. Well, there's only one way to find out who the asshole is.

IRS.

Holy shit! I have a note from the IRS tacked to my door. This cannot be good. What does the IRS want with me? I'm no one. I barely make enough money to be noticed at a wholesale club.

To: Mr. Croft
From: Alex Tuts, IRS
RE: Meeting tomorrow at 8 am.
Mr. Croft, please be at my office at 8 am.

I read this three or four times and every time the names read Tuts and Croft. No McHugh. Who's Alex Tuts? Who's Mr. Croft? Apparently, I'm okay. Looks as if someone at the IRS made a mistake. I turn to Little Jack, "Is this what you did when you got out, make trouble with the government?" It's 6:10 PM, maybe this Tuts guy has voice mail. I'll leave him a message, tell him he had the wrong house.

Blink… blink… blink. Messages. Voice messages. Now that is communication I'm comfortable with, electronic and non-destructive. "Hey Ulysses, call me when you get home, I've got great news." Oh, it's Janice. Great news, hey she probably wants to tell me how wonderful I was last night, and how she can't wait to shack up again. I think I'll have an apple first, I've got to keep my strength up to please my lady friend, then I'll call her after I call Mr. Tuts.

I love apples. I love apple sauce and apple cider. Apple pie and ice cream is also high on my list. My shampoo even smells like apples. I never really liked Matt Damon until he said, "Do you like apples? How do you like them apples?"

I dial the number on Mr. Croft's appointment tacked-mail from Mr. Tuts.

Ring…ring…ring…ring…ring (shouldn't that pick up after four

47

rings?) ring…ring (I'll give it three more) ring…"Hello." The voice on the other end is quick and harsh.

"Hi," I say pleasantly. I'm in a great mood tonight. "I'm calling for a Mr. Tuts."

"He's not here, please call back in the morning." The voice on the other end is very agitated. Obviously this guy did not get laid last night.

"Maybe you can help me, he left a note on my door…" I'm cut off.

"Sir," the voice booms through. "Sir, I just told you Tuts is not here right now, and you'd be better off calling in the morning."

That's the problem, this guy Tuts has a morning appointment with this guy Croft. I won't be able to call until I get to work, around 9 o'clock. I ask, "Do you work with him?"

The voice is getting very agitated now. "Sir, if you would just call back in the morning, you can talk to Tuts then. Right now it's late, and I am trying to go home now, so if you don't mind, call back in the morning."

I'm getting a little peeved now. Here I am just doing something nice for two total strangers, and this guy is giving me an attitude. "I appreciate that, friend, but you see I don't know what this is all about…." I'm cut off again.

"That is why you need to talk to Tuts," the jerk snaps, "I cannot help you, sir." And he hangs up. How rude. I'm fuming. That guy just flipped my most excellent attitude into rage. I can't believe how much of a jerk he was. I'm pacing around the apartment, and before I know it I grab a baseball sitting on my couch and practically start rubbing the laces off.

"What an asshole," I say out loud, as if a chorus of sympathizers are going to agree. I grab the phone to call Janice, but instead of her number, I hit redial. This knob just put me in a piss-poor mood, while I tried to do something nice. On the sixth ring he answers. "Hi, I just talked to you two minutes ago, and listen, I just want to tell this guy Tuts he has the wrong house."

"Sir," the voice is deliberate and slow this time, "if you want to talk to Tuts you'll have to call back in the morning. He has gone home and frankly that is what I'm trying to do right now, so if you don't mind…."

This time I cut him off. "Look friend, Tuts left a message for some guy Croft at my door. He left it at the wrong door. As a matter of fact, there is no Croft in the building. I'm trying to tell you that Tuts has the wrong house."

48

"Sir," he says 'sir' as if he implies to treat me with respect, "if you call Mr. Tuts tomorrow morning you can clear it up with him. Right now I'm trying to finish off my work and go home."

"Hey, I know you are trying to go home," I state obviously, "and if you took my message a few minutes ago you'd be on your way right now. Do you work with the guy Tuts?"

After a pause, just long enough to contemplate what I just said, my friend reached the epiphany I've been pulling for him to achieve, "Yes."

"Can you leave him a message?" I ask calmly.

"Fine. What is it?"

Finally, my chance to be heard. "Tell Tuts he left a tacked-mail to meet with a Mr. Croft at 8 AM tomorrow, but that no Mr. Croft lives here."

Now prepare for the second dumbest question that has ever been asked to me, "Are you sure?"

What does he mean, am I sure? It's a one bedroom apartment, I think I would have noticed this Croft guy. "Yes, I'm sure, I live alone, and I've lived here for over a year. There is not even a Croft on the mailbox for my building."

I've got him, but he's not giving up that easy, "How do you know he didn't live there before you?"

Now I don't know if this Croft guy lived here or not, I do know it was an older Italian couple who lived here before me, but Croft does not sound familiar. "I'm pretty sure."

"So you are not Croft."

He can be taught! "No, I'm not. And your Mr. Tuts left a note for Mr. Croft at the wrong address, therefore, Mr. Croft most likely will not be there in the morning for his 8 o'clock appointment."

The voice on the other end of the phone is still agitated, but beaten, "And what is your name, sir?"

"None of your business, but it's not Croft. Have a good night." As I hang up the phone, I can almost hear the voice saying thank you to me, maybe it wasn't thank you, but it was "something" you. I'll assume it was thank you.

Screw the rest of the apple, I need a beer before I call Janice.

Beer in hand, I call. "Janice, what's the great news?"

Janice is excited. "You'll never believe what the S.O.B. did today. He got fired, and his person he was going to make manager wasn't offi-cially hired, so the job went to me."

I'm happy for her. It's something she wanted.

She continues, "The only problem is I have to work weekends."

I didn't see how that was a problem at first, because right now she works weekends. It actually always worked out for us. She worked Friday nights and Saturday days, giving me a chance to hang out with my friends after work on Friday, and recover Saturday morning and afternoon to see her Saturday night. Wait. That was the assistant's schedule. "Do you mean you have to work Saturday nights now instead of days?"

"Yes," she replies timidly.

I see it coming, "Well, can you get the Saturday night off for the party?"

She replies as if she had planned for this question. I'm sure she's already had this conversation with herself. "Well, that would be my first weekend alone, without a trainer. And I have no one who can cover."

I should just hang up. "No one can cover, you guys close at eight. The party starts at eight, just come here after and we'll be there by nine."

What she says next speaks volumes to me. "It hard to say eight. I have a lot of responsibility now. I have to close the draw, lock the gates, and deposit the money." She could have stopped there, but she continued. "And I have to get home to feed the cats, and that's in an entirely different direction from you."

She has two cats. Both can live off their fat for months. She is making excuses. She works at a Sunglass Hut. I've never seen it busy there, I don't know how they stay open. How much money does she have to count? It's a Sunglass Hut. I'm fuming. She did it again. Okay, I'm ending this now. I'll tell her what she can do with her store, and her cats. "You know Janice, that's okay. Why don't you just forget about the party. I'll rescind the invitation." I can't believe it. I want to go off on her, but I just went easy on her. When will the stupidity end?

"Thanks Ulysses, I knew you'd understand. I'll call you tomorrow." And she hangs up.

That was that. My plan of friendly sex and an uncommitted relationship is over. I will never talk to that bitch again. She knew this was important to me. Where's that IRS guy's number, I'm looking for a fight. No, I can't call him. I can't call anyone. Flip and Jonathan can never know about this. I'll say she got hit by a car, and forgot about the party. I'll say her aunt died. I'll say…she's a bitch. They won't question that. I need another beer.

I don't often go to the Snow House

alone, but tonight I thought it would be okay. Then again, I'm working on two hours sleep and I'm just off two ridiculously frustrating phone calls. Oh yeah, and all I've had tonight is a beer and an apple.

The place is dead. There is a total of five people and one bartender-no waitress anywhere to be seen. I'm hoping that the night will make up for the day, but unfortunately, mistakes just keep piling up.

So, Mistake Number One, coming to the bar alone. I have no support team with me to help set up an approach, although I'm not thinking about meeting anyone, but conversely I have no one to bail me out if an undesirable steps towards me.

Mistake Number Two, I don't sit at the corner. My view is limited. My senses and instincts are now fallible. How do I know this? Well, as I said there are five people here aside from the bartender. An older couple, neither talking to the other, both staring at the TV, and three ladies who look like they are in the wrong place. Granted I'm here, but I came in jeans and a T-shirt, not in my work clothes. This is not a tie place. These three just came from work. They have on their smart clothes. They all have attractive faces, but two of them are definitely grasping onto their youth. From left to right, the first woman is about 40, short dark hair, lots of make-up, wearing a low-cut blouse, and business jacket, seated, and having a wine. I don't know what kind, I didn't even know this place had wine. Her skin is rather wrinkly. There is actually a wrinkle at the top of her breast. A decade ago I bet she was hot, now she's leather.

The second woman is standing, she's a little younger, maybe a year or two, but that's all. She too is wearing a low cut blouse with lots of make-up, but in lieu of leathery wrinkles, she has an ascot around her neck. I hate those things. What is she hiding? One time I made the mistake of not being honest with a girlfriend when she wore an ascot and every time after that she wore a new one. I painted myself into a corner. I said I liked them, a simple lie to make her feel good, and bang, there they were on all the time. Luckily my relationship with this girl ended a few weeks later when she commented on my maturity. She said sometimes talking to me is like talking to a two year old. I responded by

51

saying there are no two year olds with my vocabulary. That was our last conversation.

Anyway, the third woman, also seated, is much younger. She has on a blouse with full coverage. Her hair is shoulder length, and she's wearing little make-up. No cleavage at all. No ascot. No wrinkles. Her face is a round and chubby, but not un-cute.

I order a beer and just sit. I'm trying to relax. My eyes are closed, I'm taking deep breaths, and I'm calming down. "HA HA HA," I hear from across the bar. So much for relaxing. Leather must have told a witty story because ascot and round face are practically dying from the laughter. Suddenly, without warning, they all look at me. I think they were surprised to see me already reacting to their laughter because they all look, then as if on cue turn their heads down and away, still laughing. They were making fun of me and I caught them. How bad am I supposed to feel tonight? I turn my body to the side and finish my beer. I won't be made fun of by strangers, and I won't let them interfere with me and a beer, especially not at my bar. I will finish my beer, I will relax, and then I will go home.

With one gulp to go, I feel a tap on my shoulder. As I turn, I notice there are only two women across the bar now. The third one, younger, no cleavage, no ascot, round chubby face, is tapping me. First impressions are big, and my first impression is she doesn't have a chubby face, she has chubby everything. Oh, and now that she's not sitting, she's shorter. A chubby, short woman is tapping my shoulder. Why? "Hi, can I help you?" Hopefully she just needs directions.

"My friends and I couldn't help but notice you were looking over at us." I was looking at them? "Do you mind if I sit?"

Mistake Number Three. "No, go ahead." I am under attack...

She puts her drink on the bar, pulls out a stool, and places both hands on the seat. One leg straddles back and catches a foot rest under the stool, she leans back, lifting her 4 foot 6 inch frame just high enough to get up and nearly attain eye-level. "I'm Maria, like the ship, Santa Maria." Do I really need a metaphor to remember the name Maria? Her speech is slightly slurred. She's been here for a couple. I reach in my front right pant pocket; come on rock, get me out of this.

Mistake Number Four, "I'm U..." wait, I'm not giving her my name, she's trying to pick me up. That ain't happening. "I'm Uker. Ted Uker.

Like the ship." What that means I don't know, but I'm going to have some fun. Mistake number four averted. The count stands at three.

She speaks, "Nice to meet you, Ted. I'm Maria. Oh, you know that." The bartender comes over and asks her if she wants another. He hands me a fresh beer, just to keep me here longer. I don't know if it was his idea, or the two friends, but I can't let it go to waste. Alright Maria, you have as long as this beer. I'm not friends with the bartender, but he knows what's happening, and he's loving it. Maria says she's all set. "My friends said I should just come over here and talk to you. That you are just a person, and I'm just a person, and I should just talk to you." Good advice, I think to myself. "Also, that you have been looking over at us all night."

All night? I'm not even done with my first beer. I'll fix that. Mistake number four, though earlier averted, comes next—I enter into a conversation. After all, I have to finish my new beer, and I hate being rude. "So Maria, what do you do?"

"I'm in banking." No doubt she's a teller, probably the drive-through.

"Banking, huh? That's interesting," as if I care.

She thinks she's making strides, "Oh yeah, I meet interesting people, and I handle a lot of money."

I interrupt. "Do you ever bring your work home?" She laughs hysterically; I chuckle at her.

"No, you mean take the money? No, I can't do that." She says with conviction. "What do you do?"

Hmm, what do I do… Murderer, assassin, arsonist, plastic surgeon specializing in liposuction, what shall it be? How about inventor? Yes, inventor. "I'm an inventor. I invent."

"How interesting, anything I know?" she says, intrigued.

Yes, a dildo. "Actually, have you seen the dashboard dust monster?" She looks perplexed. "It's a stuffed, fluffy animal on a string that moves along a runner that's placed under the front windshield in your car. When you take turns, the monster slides back and forth, dusting your dash. When it gets too dirty, you throw it into the washing machine."

Her mouth is dropping, "Fascinating, it collects dust."

"That's actually our tag line: The Dash Board Dust Monster, It Collects Dust." This is fun. I tell her I've also invented the Bar-B-Q Belt

Buddy, the Travel Golf Club, and currently I'm working on a portable power generator for home electronics; how it works is while you watch TV, and the TV is plugged into the generator, you do sit-ups to keep the power on. She is absolutely in awe. I go on to tell her that Tom Selleck and Fran Drescher are going to do infomercials for me. She thinks she's found her sugar-daddy.

"Can I ask why you are here?" she asks.

I can only assume she means this bar, she doesn't seem the type to care about my id. I tell her that I am visiting my twin brother who lives in a half-way house around here. I ask if she's ever seen him here.

"This is my first time at the Snow House." I must make it her last. Anyway, I tell her I was visiting my brother and he told me about the murder the other day in the Snow House's parking lot. A yet to be solved murder, of a woman (who had a striking resemblance to Maria)—short, shoulder-length hair, size 12. There are no suspects.

"Oh my goodness, really?" As if I'm going to tell her I'm lying. "Yeah, this isn't a safe part of town," I say. After another minute or so, I've worked Maria up to the point that she no longer wants to stay here. "Well, I think maybe I should go. Will you walk me to my car?" I'm perplexed by this question because she does have two friends with her. Except that when I do a quick inventory, it seems the two friends stepped out rather casually. What am I supposed to do, say no?

I pay my tab and I walk her out. I'll have to be sure to walk right back in so the bartender doesn't think anything happened. Again, I've been here many times in the past, the bartender is not a friend, but he knows me. The last thing I need is for him to think I'm easy prey for the fat girls. I get to her car, an '86 Firebird. Can she be cheesier? I bet she has blocks on the pedals. I watch her fumble through her bag, attempt to grab her keys, and drop them. As she reaches for them on the ground, she bangs her head on the car. You'd think someone so close to the ground could pick things up easier. "Oh, that stung." She didn't get the keys, but she managed to prop herself back up and grab me. "Oops, thank you." She thanks me as if I did something. I'm just standing here. Suddenly, she runs her fingers through my hair. I'm feeling uncomfortable. Shouldn't she be afraid of the unknown killer in this parking lot? "You have nice hair."

"Thanks, let me get those." I grab her keys and as I hand them over

I realize she can't drive. I cannot let her drive. Shit. "Maria, you are in no shape to drive."

"Do you want to take me home?" What does that mean, her home or mine? Same answer, no. Think, think Ulysses. Okay, answer.

"How far do you live?" I ask.

"Just a couple of miles, in the next town," she's quick to answer. I'm too responsible to let her go on her own, but she is not getting in my car.

"I'll follow you. If you hear a horn, or I high-beam you, pull it together." I was pretty proud of myself. I was thinking quick, doing my best to make up for my recent mistakes. I'm sure driving her would be the best course of action, but I don't see that happening. I could just see her making a move on me while I drive. She'll make me swerve in fear, hit a tree. The EMT's will show up and find us locked in an embrace. A shiver runs up, then down, then up my spine again.

"Can I give you my number?" She's aggressive.

"Let's wait till I get you home." I have every intention of watching her pull into a driveway, or parking lot, and continuing straight. Bah-bye, Maria.

We get into our respective cars, and pull onto the road. Now I can't condone drunk driving, but come on, it was either this or fighting her off from the same car. The sooner she's home, the happier I'll be.

After about two miles, the inner-city strife surrounding the Snow House is replaced with a quiet farm town. We're driving along a rather abandoned road, no problems, then I see the police car. He's parked on the side of the road. The speed limit is 30, we're doing about 40, 42. I slow down, but she keeps cruising. If she gets pulled over, I'm gone. She can blame her friends. I didn't get her drunk. I only put her in the car. Half of me thinks I should floor it, distract the cop, get myself pulled over, and let her continue on. But what am I thinking? The other half, the more vocal half says she's nothing to me. A stranger I've done nothing but lie to. Now if it was Jonathan, or Flip, or Ranger-girl that's one thing. Ranger-girl, I haven't thought of her for a little while. Anyway, survival of the fittest. She's on her own.

We proceed past the cop, I'm about five seconds behind her, nice and casual. As we pass, I'm a little nervous. We look ok, but she's going too fast. "Please don't be a dick, please don't be a dick and pull us over." I stare in my rearview mirror for about 100 yards; we made it. I put my eyes back on the road just in time to notice Maria taking a right onto a dirt road and barely slamming my brakes to avert an accident. If I had hit her we would have to exchange papers, and she would know who I really am, and where I really live… not a good thing. I follow her right, and boom, Mistake Number Five.

It's not a dirt road, it's a driveway. Shit. She stops, jumps out of the car, and waddles right over to me. I stay in my car, engine running, window half-down. "Thanks, want to come in?"

Hmm, I could easily have sex, at least blow job, but do I want that? Jesus, what am I thinking? I just had it last night, so there's no urgency, and I haven't been drinking that much. "You know, I'd love to, but I have an early flight tomorrow, back to the research lab in…" this has to be somewhere good, "…Buenos Aires."

She's taken by surprise. "Lab? Buenos Aires?"

"Oh, I didn't tell you, I'm only in the States for today, I have to go back to work. Inventing is a full time, 24/7/365 job. And you go where they are inventing. Buenos Aires." I almost feel bad.

"Well, take this." It's her business card; her last name is Crane. On the back of the card is a phone number and e-mail address written in pen. "The e-mail address is different now, it's not 'thesantamaria74@yahoo.com' anymore, it's 'likesantamaria@yahoo.com.' Will you remember that, or should I write that down too?" Oh, I'll remember it. She has her e-mail already handwritten on the back of her business card. She probably has to get these out quick before her mark realizes what he's getting. "Call me when you get back," she says. I grab the card as she leans in for what I can only guess is a goodbye kiss. I don't think so. Her lips met my rising windshield. She bounces back, I hit reverse, and head home. I look at the card, shrug, and toss it into my backseat. Laughter sets in. I wish someone, anyone, could have enjoyed all that with me. It was kind of fun; sure it was at Maria's expense, but she won't remember any of that stuff. I hope not. I actually told her about my closet inventions, true they only exist in my head, but it's my head. Now she knows about them. "Ah, she won't remember a damn thing."

After a quick stop at the Snow House to proclaim nothing happened, I head home—time to sleep. It's been a long week.

Did I mention Flip is a nut? Two weeks prior

to our trip he asks me to go to the mall with him and pick up a few things. He wants to buy Dusty a gift, something she'll really like. That's why I'm with him. He knows he's a nut, and he knows he could never pick a nice gift. Flip would see nothing wrong with giving her a tool belt, or a box of condoms. Though he'll never admit it, I'm here to center him and infuse a little reality. Scary thought.

The mall's somewhat crowded today. It's two weeks before turkey day and the early Christmas shoppers are out. Unless you want to park a mile away, parking is a bitch. Fortunately, we spot a car pulling out about fifty feet away, not far from the doors. Flip hits his blinker and waits for this minivan to pull out. As they are pulling back, another car from the other direction enters the picture. Surely they must see our blinker. The minivan pulls towards us, blocking us from the spot, and that other car, a red corvette, jumps in. I look at Flip, and I figure he's going to flip out on the guy. Even the minivan lady shakes her head. How rude.

As Flip pulls forward, I roll down my window. I have a few things to say too, like, "Merry Christmas, asshole." Or, "Does your mother know what kind of dick-head she raised?" We approach the car, the person's getting out, and we keep driving.

"We're not stopping?" I ask. This is big. This is maturity. Way more than I've ever given him credit for. Way more than I have myself.

"What's the point? He won't move. Besides, I've decided I need to handle my rage better," Flip calmly explains. He drives on, turning away from the chaos and finding a nice spot towards the back. Now we have to walk. We both get out and walk a few feet when he says, "Hang on, I forgot something."

Flip runs back to the car, open the driver side door and lean towards the glove compartment. Must be his checkbook. He gets out, puts something in his coat pocket, and then we walk.

I talk about, of all things, work. "What I don't get is why Kristen and Donna want to work weekends? They finish their work on time every day. It's a little sloppy, but for the most part it's right. They have no special projects to work on. Donna's been trained, and seems okay on her own, although I guess she's never on her own, her and Kristen always take the same days off." That's when I notice where we are, "Hey, isn't that the car that took our spot?"

As I turn to ask Flip, I see that he too noticed the car, and he is halfway through his delivery of what turned out to be an egg. Crash/splat. He just nailed the back window with an egg.

"Jesus Christ! What are you doing?" I exclaim.

"Handling my rage," he says flatly as he starts walking to the driver side door and reaches into his pocket for another egg. "I figured what goes around, comes around. I'm just pushing things in a direction I think they should naturally, organically take." With that he jams the egg under the door handle. Say what you will, I think it's beautiful. Flip grins. "That's what you get for finding such a great spot." He then steps away and pulls a little notebook out of his pocket, and as we walk away he writes something down.

"What are you writing?" I ask.

"Oh, I'm adding that guy's car to my shit-list," he informs me.

A shit-list. That's awesome. Is there any wonder this guy's one of my best friends?

We head right for the Bath and Body Works store, ironically just two stores away from Sunglass Hut. I hope the manager is on today. As we enter, I'm overwhelmed by the aroma. Soap and shampoo for women. Is it any wonder why they smell so much nicer than men? I can't shop here. Good old Irish Spring for me.

The plan is to look lost, and wait for help. In a store full of eighteen to thirty-four year old women, Flip and I stand out. I think having us in here may be bad for business. Within thirty seconds we hear, "Can I help you with anything?" The name tag reads Britney. She looks like a Britney. Seventeen years old, and smells oh so nice. She has long curly brown hair with blond streaks. Tall, cute, and boy, can she fill out a sweater. Why didn't girls look like this when I was in high school? I direct her to Flip through the art of pointing.

He starts, "I need to find something nice for my girlfriend." I mildly snicker. Girlfriend. Whatever makes him happy. I'm afraid now if I aggravate him that there may be a spot on the shit-list for me.

Britney is up for the challenge, "Okay, what does she like?"

58

"I don't know, she lives in Minnesota, oh, and she has a wonderful tan," Flip answers.

Britney gives him a look then takes him over to the moisturizers. I wander over to the back massagers. They look so goofy, like round little alien dogs. I pick one up and start rubbing my shoulders. I turn to find Flip and see Janice walking right over to me. The last thing I need.

"Hey stranger," she starts. "I haven't seen you for a while, I've been so busy."

She hasn't seen me because she's the one that's been busy. "Yeah, I've been busy too, planning my trip, and helping with Jonathan and Dany's party." Maybe that should ring a bell, the party that her fat cats took precedence over.

"Yeah, I feel bad about that. What do you say I take you out for lunch tomorrow afternoon?" she asks.

Oh, that will make up for it. "No, actually, I'm busy. I don't think I'll be able to make lunch," I say.

"How about dinner this week?"

"It's a tough week." Then, as if on cue, Flip walks up.

"Hi Janice, nice to see you again." He's so fake.

"Hi Flip, you shop here?" she says, with an equally fake amount of care.

"Oh yeah, nothing like mango shampoo. Ulysses, don't you owe me a drink?" Flip replies.

"Well, I have to get to work. I'll talk to you later, Ulysses. Bye Flip." She leaves.

"Thank you Flip. And no, I do not owe you a drink." I'm very happy he came when he did. Janice has tried to call me twice in the last week, and both times I've not answered the phone. I've also received a couple of e-mails, but they have been joke e-mails. Nothing to me directly, no apologies, nothing. This lunch thing is new, obviously the sex is so good she is trying to keep in my good graces. Good luck.

"Check it out man, mango shampoo, coconut soap, citrus conditioner, and a sponge to apply, and one of those cool massage alien dogs. I think that can double as a sexual toy," he says smiling.

"Yeah, you are a lucky man, Flip." I say as we head out. On the way to the car Flip comments to me how he thinks the Bath and Body girl had a thing for him. I told him we'll go back next month if things between him and Dusty don't work out.

As we get in the car and head towards the exit, Flip turns down the row with the red corvette and wouldn't you know someone is holding a bunch of food court napkins trying to remove egg from his back window. Good thing he saved all that time in the mall by finding such a peach of a spot.

"Son-of-a-Bitch, it's cold," I say as I step out of my warm car and wrap my scarf around my face, "Cold, cold, cold, cold, cold." Actually, cold doesn't begin to describe 25 degrees in mid-November. I'm waiting at the station for my train, but on days like today, the wait always seems longer in the cold. This week, and next, at work is going to be so dull. I think the world is looking forward to the break a long Thanksgiving weekend provides. Yes, I know the world doesn't celebrate Thanksgiving, that it is only a US holiday, but when your world centers around a thirty mile radius of Boston, then excuse me for taking broad liberties in holiday assessment.

Labor Day was such a long time ago, and everyone has had enough of work since the last long weekend. Did I mention how cold it is today? There is absolutely no visible flesh on anyone. Ranger-girl could be a half dozen other people here at the train stop. From head to toe, not one commuter is without hats, long coats, gloves and boots. Why did my family settle here?

The train finally comes, the doors open, and there is heat, happy heat. Everyone starts shedding layers. Slowly, faces emerge. Familiar faces of the people I travel with daily. There's the Hoochy-girl. She's about twenty-two, twenty-three years old. One day I sat next to her and had the pleasure of watching the performance art she calls putting on her make-up. I know, you have to save time and cut corners wherever and whenever you can, but every day she does her make-up on the train. And it's not just eye-liner. It goes: base, rouge, mascara, eye-liner, lipstick, and lip-liner. Then the jewelry comes. Ear rings, finger rings, one for each finger, including thumbs, and necklaces. This is what she does the whole ride.

The first day I saw her, I thought she might be cute, but the illusion was shattered when I saw the process to get there. Recently she has been showing a little belly. Pregnant or not, thumb rings go on.

There is this guy: dirty, grungy, smelly. I was told by one of the conductors that they call him the Ham-burglar. What this name means I'm not sure, but I guess every day he tries to sneak on without paying. He's been kicked off several times, and when a conductor approaches him, he sometimes tries to speak a different language, to throw the con-

conductor off. Word is he travels to the dog track daily. No wonder I never go to the dog track.

Across from me is The Couple. He's my age, she's at least 40. She clearly dictates the relationship. His dress is very casual compared to hers, which is a bit frumpy. Nothing seems to fit her right. Everything is a pant suit. She has short red hair that she wears parted to the side like Richie Cunningham, not a good look for older women. The entire ride, she talks. Usually about how he should confront his boss, or volunteer for special projects, or rat out follow co-workers. He just takes it as if he's accepted his role in life, to be her pin-cushion. Mark my words, someday he'll jump in front of a train, and may not care to make it look like an accident.

You would think after traveling together all these months that occasionally a conversation might spark between us strangers, but recently, the more I think of it, the less I want to talk to any of these people. I'm just happy Billy Dee hasn't returned.

Ranger-girl is on the train today. She has on a cute brown leather jacket that goes down just below her butt. It's tied in the middle, giving her a very curvy look. Her blond hair pokes out from under her knit Boston Red Sox hat. Today she has jeans on with little brown boots that have a furry little tongue folded over the laces. She is so damn cute.

It's fun to watch people on the train. Their mannerisms here are quite different than anywhere else—for example, in a cafeteria. On the train, no one talks to strangers. If you are not distracted by a book or walkman, your eyes stay down, or up, but never at eye level. Some people are lucky enough to travel with friends, but that can get old. Sometimes you see two people you know sit or stand together during the ride on most days, but occasionally they are nowhere near one another, in different cars, or opposite ends of the same car. It is as if they are both pretending not to see the other. And if by accident they do catch each other's eye the only response is, "Oh, there you are, I didn't see you." That's what you get when you don't distract yourself via walkman, book, or other means.

I stopped carrying books or my walkman. I used to, but it became too stressful. I swear, people try to read books over your shoulder. It drives me crazy. And as for the walkman, I hate dealing with the wires. And I go through a small fortune in batteries; no matter what I try, they run out of juice at the end of the week. It's not worth it. So now, I cross my arms, and pretend to sleep. Sitting or standing, my eyes are closed, and usually people leave me alone. There might be a better way to avoid people on the train, but until I can figure it out, this is my new approach.

You can always tell when the train is hitting a big station stop, like for connecting trains, or the financial district. About two minutes before the train arrives, the runners get ready. I call them the runners because that is what they do. Once the door opens, boom, they are out the door and hustling big time to wherever. Not me, I'm in no rush. These people can be so rude. They "excuse me," "pardon me," their way to the door, cutting in front of anyone in their way, only to wait. If I liken the commute to a rodeo, with so many cattle in the train cars, the runners are the bull riders. The gate opens, they're wrestling, and maneuvering, and within eight seconds it's over. That's all the runners need to break away, and be the first wherever.

As for the rest of us, it's a slow pace to the door, along the track, up the stairs, and out the station. From that point things break up nicely. There are about a dozen different ways to get anywhere in Boston, and with all the construction those ways change daily. I usually walk along this one building on Federal Street that has a Starbucks inside. I like to check out the patrons—Dunkin' Donuts has better coffee, but Starbucks has cuter coffee drinkers.

As I round the corner of the building, I'm presented with the skyline of Boston. New York might have 100 times as many skyscrapers, and L.A. might have that yellow–orange haze, but Boston has its history and the waterfront. Every building, in its own way, is a piece of art. No cookie cutter designs here, no sir, there is a lot of style packed into this small city. They may not be the tallest in the world, but there is no way you'd ever get me to clean the windows of one of those "smaller" 50 story monoliths.

I always look up at the first sight of the skyscrapers. It's as if I'm walking in a forest of glass and steel. I like to imagine what it was, and still is like to build one of these giants. And not only build them, but then put something inside. Not to mention clearing land in a very densely populated zone, and during construction not dropping heavy things onto passers-bys' heads.

I can't look up for too long for two reasons: One, I don't want to look like a tourist. Tourists get mugged, and I don't want to get mugged. Sure there are 40,000 other people walking to work at the same time I am, but still, I want credit for belonging, and two, you've got to watch your step. Too much construction. That sidewalk that was there yesterday may not be there today, or tomorrow. Also, there are some people you don't want to accidentally bump. For example, those who are bigger than you.

Fortunately today, I looked down just in time to catch some side-walk theatre. Today's performer is a business woman reading a small piece of paper, and looking up frequently. She doesn't belong. Her hair is up, and she's wearing a gray overcoat with a black pant suit, and sneakers. Old sneakers. She has a purse and a bag, a bag large enough for shoes. The performance starts innocently enough, she's looking at her paper, and then up at the street signs. She must have an interview. Suddenly, a personal Nor'easter decides to come down on her. A gust of wind hits her, and catches the paper, sending it up into the air, then down to the ground in a whoosh. She gives chase, only to be teased by the wind. As she gets close, the paper whooshes away again. I can almost hear the theme music from Benny Hill. Finally, she gets it with her foot. As she goes to bend and grab the paper, more wind comes, and flop, her hair comes undone. Poor lady; it's not even 9 o'clock yet.

I walk past her as she is trying to compose herself. "Is this Federal Street?" she asks.

"Yes, all the way to the corner." I'm glad to bring a little aid to her struggle. As we go our separate ways, I see this guy, about my age, a little older, wearing a jean jacket, scarf, and khakis. He's laughing to himself. I think we both enjoyed today's performance.

Within five minutes, I'm in front of the Armstrong building, look-ing for my ID badge. Did I mention it's too cold to be fumbling around my person looking for this stupid badge? Once in hand, a quick swipe and, thankfully, I'm where the heat is. It might be work, but it's warm. The train, the woman with the paper and the guy in the jean jacket are behind me. Why can't I make a career out of watching people? I'd en-joy it more than this place.

Ah, there are my boys, Clint and Charles. "Good morning gentle-men, it's a cold day out. I hope those thermoses are full of some good stuff," I say in a very condescending tone as I point to their flashlights.

64

How could I mistake a flashlight for a thermos, oh I have so much to learn from these two.

"Hang on one minute," Clint approaches me. "It's Ulysses, right? Did you sign this?"

Clint hands me a memo. It's the authorization memo I wrote so Kristen and Donna can get into the building on weekends. "Yes, what's wrong?"

"We were doing our rounds on Saturday," Clint informs me, "and we caught these two having a grand old time, laughing, running, jumping, real excited. Are they coming here to work, or play?"

If only he knew who he was talking about. I don't care for Kristen or Donna, but Clint and Charles tend to overreact. I assure him that I'll talk to them, and I head for the elevator.

"We'll need a new letter stating why they are here on the weekends." Clint yells toward me as I step into the elevator. I casually acknowledge him with a wave. Do I need this?

Like clockwork, Flip and Jonathan are waiting for me by Flip's desk. As I approach, Jonathan seems a little more animated than usual. I insert myself into the conversation with, "Already had some coffee today, I see."

Jonathan turns to me, "Hey Ulysses, I was just telling Flip that Dany and I went to the movies last night, to see that Uma Thurman movie, and the tickets were $8.50 each."

Obviously Jonathan has not been to the movies in a while, not since Return of the Jedi anyway. "Yeah, so?"

"Uma Thurman…It cost me seventeen bucks to see her cry for 90 minutes." His animations increase. "When did movies become so expensive?"

Flip jumps in, "Maybe if you have been to one in the last ten years."

"But for Uma Thurman crying," Jonathan reacts. "Maybe I'd spend seventeen bucks to see the death star blown up again, but it's Uma Thurman. Crying."

I see his point. "Jonathan, why did you see that movie anyway? Lose a bet?" He nods yes.

Flip steps forward, "I'll never see another Uma Thurman movie again. She on my shit-list." He says this looking right at me. When I go home I might have to jump online and see if Uma has ever been egged.

65

"Why is she on your shit list?" I ask.

"Two words, Batman & Robin," Flip proclaims, with mild rage.

"That's three," Jonathan adds.

Flip holds up his left hand and extends his thumb, "Batman," then he extends the index finger, "Robin."

Jonathan just looks at him and extends his middle finger, "And…what's and? "And" is a word."

Flip counters, "Not if it's an asterisk!"

I jump back in. "You mean ampersand."

"What?" Flip obviously noticed my second head. "Amper-what?"

"The little squiggly line over the seven." I point to his keyboard. "Ampersand."

"Well, it's still not a word, it's a character." Flip walks off. Jonathan and I follow yet Jonathan does not relent.

"Isn't a character just in substitution for a word in print? You wouldn't read Batman ampersand Robin, its Batman AND Robin," Jonathan says.

I pipe in, "Why is Uma Thurman on your shit list for Batman ampersand Robin?" Jonathan and I chuckle.

Flip stops and looks at us both. "Have you seen Batman & Robin? I know you haven't," as he looks in Jonathan's direction, "It is one of the worst movies ever. And I blame Uma Thurman, Alicia Silverstone, and Joel Schumacher. Those three ruined the Batman movies, and for that they are all on my shit list, and I will never again see any of their movies. Even if they are in the new Star Wars, I will not see it. They'll just ruin that too."

I ask, "You blame them for Batman. What about George Clooney and Arnold?"

"Two words," again the thumb. "Poor," and the index finger, "direction." He continues. "When I'm out in Hollywood, I'll make it part of my agenda to make sure those three never work again."

We both wanted to know, but Jonathan got it out first. "Hollywood, when are you going to Hollywood?"

Flip smiles, "It's all part of my plan."

Enough said. Now Jonathan and I continue walking, and leave Flip to catch up with us. We turn a corner towards the elevator, and down on the floor in tight blue jeans and a green apron is a beautiful brunette, with her hair pulled back in a ponytail, wearing really thin glasses, and she's stretching across the floor watering the plants along the wall. Nice butt. I slow, and nudge Jonathan, "Whoa."

"Whoa," he says under his breath as he catches a glimpse.

Then Flip turns the corner. "Whoa, plant girl." Nothing discreet about that. She looks up and smiles at him. Flip continues on his way to the elevator leaving a smile and a wink for "plant-girl". When the door shuts, we all get a good laugh, and agree to take the stairs on the other side of the floor when we return.

Later, back at my desk, I fire off an e-mail.

To: Kristen LaGrace and Donna Kiernan

Re: Weekend work

The security team told me they came across some odd stuff on Saturday. I don't care if you guys are goofing around; just make it look like some work is getting done.

And that's all. I wanted to be stern in the e-mail. Make it look like I feel they are taking advantage of me. I'm their only friend here besides each other; they don't want to be on my bad side. Send.

As the letter is sent, and my mail refreshes, I see yet another Janice invite to lunch or dinner.

"Ulysses, we gotta get together. Friday? J."

Gee, Friday, I think I'm busy. I have to throw bread to the squirrels in my back yard. I send a reply:

"Sorry, I'm busy."

And that's all. No reason, no alternative schedule. I am busy. Get the point.

Not too long after I get a reply.

"I guess you are not interested in being friends, never call me again."

Wow. Harsh. When did I ever call her? Does she realize I stopped talking to her? Is this her way of breaking up with me? Does she realize you can't breakup with someone you aren't dating? "Son-of-a-Bitch, that's cold."

Wednesday, November 22nd. D-day. It seems like

Flip has been planning this thing for years. He called in sick today because of some last-minute details he had to attend to, very top secret, very hush-hush. He's got to be nervous, though he'd never say. The anniversary party this past weekend went off without a hitch. Dany was so surprised. They got there a little past 8 o'clock; Jonathan told her they were going to a Thanksgiving work party. Who has a Thanksgiving work party? Certainly not North Union, but then again, she bought it. At first she saw Flip and I, but then once her folks walked up, and Jonathan's parents came over, and she saw the cousins and aunts and uncles, she was overwhelmed. The first thing out of her mouth was, "I'm pregnant." Well, that sent everyone into hysterics, suddenly it was all family. Flip and I headed to the bar and had a few beers. Luckily, the Celtics were on.

By ten o'clock, we had congratulated the two of them. Dany kissed me on the lips, but only hugged Flip. Granted, it was only a peck on the lips, not to mention she's married to one of my best friends and pregnant, but coming from Dany I'll take it. I think Flip was happy to get the hug. We didn't last too long; it was a big family night.

I figure today I'll start sending people home at two, mainly because I want to get home myself. One person will have to stay until five, I think that will be Kristen. She owes me. She apologized for that weekend she and Donna were goofing around in the office. I told her the office is for work, and I hoped it didn't happen again. I tried to be stern, so they did not think they could take me for granted. Plus, if I was too nice, they might think something was up.

During the last half hour everyone is ready to leave, except Kristen. Oh and look, Donna is sticking around too. Sticking around, I'm sure they are used to that. Jonathan and I have coordinated our plans to meet up with Flip. Flip's picking us up by 3:30, no later. He's got a purple Ford Windstar. It'll be amazing if we make it there and back. Three white guys driving a purple minivan. GAY. Flip tried to tell me we'll fit in better because our minivan is the color of the Vikings, and everyone in Minnesota is fanatical about the Vikings. So fine, we'll look like gay Vikings fans.

No one wants to answer the phone right now. Any call could delay us all from leaving. If the phone rings at 2:01, too bad, but at 1:59, we stay. I imagine this is what it is like when they launch the space shuttle. Sure it's been done before, but during those last 30 minutes, you just want to blast off.

Jonathan comes over to my desk, and reads my paper. It's a slow day. 1:35, 1:40, 1:45. Fifteen minutes to go. There is absolutely no work being done right now, and we are all getting paid for it. You got to love the holidays.

Jonathan pipes up from behind the paper, "Hey, we're going to miss the parade tomorrow."

I ask, "And this bothers you?"

Casually he states, "No." Neither one of us talk for the next 13 minutes. We'll have plenty of time to talk on the ride.

1:58, almost home free, until…ring. Everyone holds their collective breath. It's Julie's desk. Julie, she's been here for five years, no one could be calling here with a problem with her work. Maybe they have a problem with someone else's work. Why is her phone ringing? We were so close. I hear her, "Hello," and there is a pause. She soon smiles and looks up to everyone, "It's my husband." A sign of relief cascades over the third floor, the threat is over.

Two o'clock, and the exodus is on. Good-bye North Union for four days. Jonathan and I get off the elevator and walk past Clint and Charles, "Have a wonderful holiday, everyone," Clint says with a smile.

"You too, keep the building safe for us, we'll be back on Monday," I offer up. He starts to say something to me after, but I really wasn't too interested. Jonathan thought I was being rude. He just does not understand our relationship.

I get off the train at 2:45; I've got enough time to get a few things together before the journey begins. As I pull out of the parking lot, there's Alice. Her face is really red today. It is cold out. All she has on is a really old Members Only jacket, jeans with a hole in the knee, and flip-flops. At least she had enough sense to wear socks with her flip-flops. She might make as much as I do, but I have the holidays off. It wouldn't surprise me if she worked all weekend.

2:50, and I'm at the apartment. I make a quick sandwich, grab my suitcase, and turn on the TV. I've got a good half hour before Flip arrives. It's funny, I'm actually looking forward to this trip. Two months ago there was no way I'd go, or rather no way I thought Flip would talk me into going. I still think it's real odd to make plans with a stranger over six months ahead of time, and not talk to that stranger the entire time, but that's Flip. These are the little adventures I've grown to expect. I better put on the Weather Channel. We are going to Minnesota and it has a reputation for snowing.

By 3:20, I hear the beep. He's early. I turn off the TV, check that the heat is turned down, make sure the toaster is not plugged in, check the faucets, grab my suitcase, tap LJ's cage and tell him, "No wild parties, your grandparents will be over tomorrow night to feed you. Be good, buddy, and don't die." Finally I grab my backpack, and head for the door. Flip meets me at the threshold. He's excited.

"Are you ready?" he screams.

"Let's roll, baby." I step out, close and lock the door behind me. As I walk to the parking lot, there it is, a purple minivan, a Windstar. We'll look so gay. I walk past my car and tap her on the hood. I'll be home soon.

The inside of the minivan is nice and spacious, as a matter of fact I don't know where I'd rather sit, shotgun or in the back. There is so much room. We dump my bags in the way-back, and Flip heads out. One thing about minivans—they are built for families. Families with two to four active kids and well-to-do parents. I don't mean to say you have to be rich to own a minivan, after all Jaguar doesn't make them, but they are far more practical than a coupe or a station wagon.

Minivans are the upper edge of the middle class in parenting. There are so many gadgets and hidden toys for all parties to use. The minivan engineers know their craft. For instance, the center console has spaces for CDs and tapes, along with a first-aid kit. There are two cup holders in the front, and two more inside the center console. There are extensions that pull out of the sun visors. Individual heat zones. And spots above your head for a garage door opener and sunglasses. This baby is cherry.

On the way to Jonathan's, Flip tells me about a hitchhiker down the street that he thought about helping out, but opted for getting on the road as early as possible. He told me she looked a bit like a skank, walking around in flip-flops. I told him he really doesn't want to pick up hitchhikers around here because you can never be sure where they've been.

71

Twenty minutes later we have Jonathan, and we are on our way. The luggage is stored tightly in the back, I'm riding shotgun, and Jonathan is spread out behind us.

"This is a cherry ride," Jonathan informed Flip and I from the back, "but purple, could we look more gay?"

I turned to Jonathan, "Wait, you haven't experienced 'Minivan' until you've explored all the options 'Minivan' has for you, such as..." I start to open all the compartments and hidden items within our cherry ride, and much to the shock of Jonathan and I, two packaged condoms fall to the floor from the sunglass holder above the center console, a place I had not earlier explored. I pick them up, first verifying they are sealed, and ask Flip, "What exactly did you have in mind for us this trip, or are these for when we arrive, stud?"

Flip had a look of surprise he was trying to sell us. "I swear those are not mine. They must have been in the car all along." He's either telling us the truth, and these condoms are left over from a previous renter, which makes me feel real uncomfortable figuring the rental agent probably does not shampoo the car seats between clients. Or, they are his and he is acting surprised. He's not that good an actor, and Flip would not lie about something as accepted in pop-culture as condom possession. I think when we stop at a rest station, I'm grabbing some paper towels from the restroom. I feel dirty.

"So how far is this trip, exactly?" I ask.

Flip looks at me briefly, "It really doesn't seem far, Minnesota really doesn't seem far at all."

"How far is it, eight hundred miles?" Flip said we'd be there by two in the morning. Ten hours of driving should get us there by two.

"A little further," Flip says.

"900 miles?" I ask.

"A little further," Flip says.

"It's not a thousand miles away, is it?" Jonathan pops in. Flip doesn't answer, he just nods. Not quite an affirmation nod, but not a negation nod either.

I grab the map sitting between the seats and study it for a few moments. "Fourteen hundred miles! There's no way we'll be there by two in the morning! We probably won't even make dinner! Hell, we'll be lucky to get there for dessert!"

Jonathan grabbed the map. He scans what I just read and reaches for Flip's shoulder. "What happened to 800 miles, the 11 hour ride tops. That's as far as Florida. And we never drive to Florida."

Flip is up against the ropes. "Hey, careful, I'm driving." Jonathan removes his hand. "Okay, it's a little further than I first assumed, but no big deal, I've got the driving down. By this time tomorrow this ride will be a memory."

"Yeah, because we will be just getting out of the car!" I exclaim. There's a little silence. I can't be sure if Flip knew how far it was all along, or if he just found out himself recently and didn't want to tell us. I'm sure he hoped we weren't just five miles into the trip before we figured this out. "Pull over up at the corner."

"What?" Flip is worried. "You're not bailing on me, are you?"

"No," I say, "But you are not driving fourteen hundred miles alone. I'll drive for a couple hours, then maybe Jonathan will, then you can have our triumphant entrance into Minnesota, maybe a couple hundred miles before. Pull over at the corner so I can get a coffee at Dunkin' Donuts."

"Sure." Flip seems okay with the new plan. He pulls into the parking lot and heads for the entrance.

"You guys want anything?" I ask.

"No," Jonathan says as he hops out of the minivan, "but I'll come with you." Flip just sits and smiles.

Once we are in the store, Jonathan asks, "Are you mad?"

"No, are you?"

"No, I actually checked it out about a month ago and been planning to hold this against him. Besides, I have nowhere to be until Monday anyway. Why not drive nearly three thousand miles for one meal, I bet they have cranberry sauce."

Flip's probably thinking we are trashing him right now. Let him think that for a while. It'll make for a quieter ride. There are four people ahead of us in line. With one of these people is this cute little girl. I'd say she's five years old. Her parent has ornamented her with a pink fluffy coat, furry cuffs, and hood. She has on corduroy pants with a little Winnie the Pooh on the side. Her sneakers also bear the mark of the Pooh. Oddly enough she's holding a carrot. I catch her eye. "I remember when I was a kid, I couldn't wait to build my first snowman of the season either." She looks at me, a little puzzled. "Nice carrot," I say. A few of the people in front laugh politely.

At this time her mother grabs her free hand and pulls her forward. "Nice job, Ulysses." Jonathan states. "Snowman, ha." He giggles. He just wishes he thought of the snowman line first. Obviously the mother wasn't too impressed, but I got a couple laughs. I'm happy with that.

The mother of the little girl is ordering, and she turns to her daughter and asks if she wants a donut. Duh, she's holding a carrot, of course she wants a donut. The little girl says she wants "that one." Everyone in line and behind the counter thinks this is pretty cute. The Dunkin Donuts employee reaches up and points to an orange and green and red sprinkled donut with chocolate frosting, "This one?" she asks.

"No, that one." The little girl seems to be pointing in the same spot, but maybe not. The girl behind the counter lowers her hand to another rack, full of powdery lemon donuts. "This one?" she asks.

"No, that one." The little girl points, again seemingly pointing to the same spot. This time the Dunkin Donuts girl moves her hand up towards the original donut, and over to the left. A rack full of honey-dipped donuts. Big brown donuts with a shinny honey glaze. "This one?" again she asks.

"No, that one." Again the finger points to the same spot, the first rack of donuts already nixed. The girl behind the counter laughs, but this is quickly losing its cuteness. The line is getting long. This time we think she points at a plain donut. No sprinkles, no glaze, no filling. "Not this one?" We all know the answer already.

"No," with a big huff; this girl wants her donut, "that one!" I wish the boys all the luck in the world, because when this one starts dating, she'll be trouble.

Here mother leans in, "Honey, are you just playing?"

"Mommy, I want the one with the colors." The little girl says on the brink of crying.

Her mother looks at the crowd behind her, "But honey, you said you don't want that one." At the same time the girl behind the counter points at the original rack of donuts again.

"I don't want that one," she says, "I want that one" and this time between the furious points, the attentive onlooker could see that there was a half degree variance between point one and point two. She doesn't want the donut that the counter girl is pointing to, on the right of the colorful sprinkle rack, she wants the one next to it just to the left, in the middle of the rack. "That one, that one."

Now we get it. The counter girl finally points to the right donut, not the rack, and packs it up into a bag for the little girl. Boom, big smile. When Jonathan and I get to the counter I get a coffee, and we both pitch in for a dozen donuts: Three with the colorful sprinkles, four lemon filled, four glazed, and one plain...for Flip.

Ten minutes later, we're on the highway, and I'm driving along Route 128 heading for Minnesota.

Back when I was in college, I would drive my car every fall to Florida, and every spring back to Massachusetts. My father would always accompany me, either flying to me, or flying home afterwards. It was a lot of fun to have a car at school, since not everyone was afforded that luxury. Who cares what it looked like, or the fact it was an old-lady Ford Escort. I had mobility, the power to travel further than my legs could walk. I drove.

It was a two-day drive down, two-day drive back. Four days that sucked every year. The New England states were ok, New York we were in and out of fast. New Jersey was long, and the further south you got, the worse the roads seemed. Delaware and Maryland were easy enough, making for a deceiving first day. Our goal was always Virginia. In all, the first day we'd travel about 600 miles, through eight states. The second half of the ride, although less miles, would seem to take twice as long. North Carolina is long. South Carolina is longer. Can you say oppressive? FYI, don't travel through South Carolina on a Sunday and hope to get a beer with lunch or dinner. Bible Belt. No beer anywhere on Sunday. One of the many reasons I'll never live in South Carolina. Then you hit Georgia. Now Georgia's a big state, but Interstate 95 only skirts the easternmost side. Still, it's two hours. Finally, Florida. It was still another two hours to St. Augustine, but being in the state made the traveling a little easier with your eyes on the prize.

One time, my junior year, we were driving through Virginia around 7 pm, twelve hours after we started. We pulled into a Holiday Inn, and they were booked solid. We'd already been driving all day, and we hadn't eaten since about 2 o'clock, with the exception of potato chips and peanuts, long-ride necessities. Well, the clerk at the Holiday Inn outside of Richmond was able to find us a room…in North Carolina. Lumberton, North Carolina. Two hundred and forty miles south of Richmond. Four more hours of driving, only thirty miles north of the South Carolina border. We drove eight hundred miles in sixteen hours. That was the longest day of my life.

It was bad enough, all the traffic driving through Baltimore, Washington DC, and Richmond, but now four more hours. My father started, and after two hours I did the last haul. Never before was I hypnotized by the road until the last hour of that ride. I was so exhausted, my father probably nudged me awake two or three times. The first time I snapped right out, same as the second. I wasn't really asleep, but I was fading. The third time I was out. Thank God Dad was awake, because I was drifting to the left. I heard "Ulysses!" and jumped to, righted the car, and sweated the whole way to Lumberton.

The only good thing about driving that long was the next day's drive was nothing. I swore I would never drive that tired again, or that far. I make enough money to buy airline tickets. If Flip had done his research, we could have flown to St. Paul; I don't care how much it cost. But he was being cheap.

I'll drive through New York, maybe through Pennsylvania, into Ohio, Jonathan can have it then. Depending on how we feel when we get there, I'll buy myself an airline ticket home.

Somewhere in New York, while traveling I-90, the New York Thruway, we hit a little town called Chittenango. Hell, it could be a huge metropolis for what I know, all I see is the highway, at night. The radio is dead, but Flip keeps scanning. Nothing is on other than a college station out of Syracuse, an easy-listening/soccer mom station, and sports radio. Frankly I can do without hearing the locals brag about the Yankees, or any of the New York teams. Well, with the exception of the Islanders; I kind of feel bad for them. They suck. The minivan has a tape deck, no CD player, a tape deck. I don't think anyone of us has bought a tape in five years. Our CDs are useless. This is already a long trip, and we're still in New York.

Flip starts making up for the lack of music by chatting. "Hey, we've been driving five hours, almost halfway there."

I look up at Jonathan in the rearview mirror. He's motioning that he'll make the initial comment. "Flip, this is a minimum twenty hour ride. How do you get that we are halfway there?"

Flip smiles, "If you sleep 10 hours, and if you are awake for ten hours, then the five hours we have done so far IS halfway, maybe a third of the way. Come on you guys, it's not that bad. Okay, it's a little longer than I first thought, but who cares? It's the three of us on the open road. We got a map, a horizon, and a destination. This is an adventure." Silence.

"I promise, we'll be there by eight in the morning," Flip says reassuringly.

"How can you promise that?" I ask.

"Trust me. When have I ever been wrong?" Flip replies.

Jonathan and I look at each other for only a moment. We decide to list, in no particular order what Flip has predicted, and been wrong about:

"In high school, Karen Kennedy from the cheerleader squad did not like you," I start, and then we both just go off:

"In college, just because your roommate gets an STD doesn't mean you automatically pass."

"Bert and Ernie are not gay lovers."

"You never slept with two women at once," evident by the fact that #8 is still unfulfilled.

"Chelsea Clinton did not flirt with you in Martha's Vineyard."

"You've never been to Martha's Vineyard."

"Cats are not on the verge of extinction."

"Oh, and Y2K." Flip had this crazy theory that all the Y2K bug stories were right. He really believed that the end of the world would be January 1st, 2000. To the degree that he bought a gun, subscribed to survival magazines, filled his basement with crates and crates of canned goods and dry food and bottled water. He thought that all the hysteria over Y2K was only a counter/counter story. In order to make people not worry about it, that the governments of the world made the problem seem big, but fixable, and that they had no worries. But in fact, the problem was so huge not only did the governments accept the fall of society, but welcomed it. They could fix everything, but choose not to, in order to re-start civilization.

Flip was sure that without the shipping of goods and services, that within nine months society would fall and anarchy would rein. He then figured that after six months of that, either plague, or food shortages would kill off the majority of people, then when the population had dwindled to a mere few, the governments would flip a switch, turning all the power back on. Those who survived would be the strong and resourceful. The ones on which a new society would grow. All the dead weight that kept the world tied up in menial problems would be gone.

This was even a little crazy for him. Usually his paranoia doesn't reach a global level, but Y2K got him. He swore that on the 31st of December he was locking himself into his basement, and no matter what would not emerge until four days later. Why four days, I don't know, but he thought that after the initial looting, by the fourth day everyone would need to rest, and that's when he'd check out to see if he was right or wrong.

As it turns out, he was over my house that afternoon. We watched TV and saw New Years happen all over the world, Australia, Japan, Hong Kong, then Asia and Europe. Seeing everything turn out okay in those areas comforted him. By nine o'clock that night he started drinking, at ten I talked him into going to a party with me, and at midnight nothing catastrophic happened, obviously.

For six straight months, Flip ate a diet of Campbell's soup and cereal.

"Okay, okay," Flip starts, "I might have been mislead, or overreacted in the past, but that was the old me. I swear, we'll be there by eight. Oh, and was I not right when I said the cigarette smoking man was Mulder's father during season three?"

"Oh, I'm sorry," I say, "Jonathan, we owe him props."

"We owe you props."

"You owe me props."

Sometime after New York, I had enough and gave Jonathan the controls. We pulled into an all night 7 Eleven, peed, grabbed a few more supplies, and drove on. I was asleep before we hit the onramp. The backseat of a minivan is not the most comfortable place in the world, but right now, you could slap me onto the luggage rack and I would still sleep.

By the time I woke up, I felt like I had been asleep for a month. It may not be a pretty minivan, but it is surprisingly comfortable. I wonder where we are. My eyes have not adjusted to the world yet. I'm still in the just-waking-up state of mind when two-foot pink elephants in lederhosen seem plausible to me. The highway markers look like they say Minnesota, but right now they could say Jupiter and I couldn't read it. Flip's driving, hands at ten and two, and Jonathan is passed out next to him in front. I can barely make out the time on the clock. 9:66, no. 9:88, no 9:58, I have to rub my eyes. 7:58. Wow, it's almost eight o'clock and we are in Minnesota. I don't know how he did it, but I'm impressed. I reach out and grab his shoulder, "Good job man, you did it."

Flip screams and almost pulls us into a guardrail. "Holy shit, what did you do that for!" he yells at me. When he turns I can see his face. There is perspiration running down his face. His t-shirt is soaked. His eyes are totally bloodshot. Maybe it's a good thing I slept the entire ride. The speedometer says ninety-five. Jonathan is still asleep.

"Please tell me you haven't been driving that fast the entire time. Are you crazy?" I ask.

"Fine, I won't tell you, but we are twenty minutes out of St. Paul, and in forty minutes we'll be in the hotel. Complain all you want, but we're here." Flip has a smile of accomplishment across his face. At least 95 miles an hour, for at least seven hours. I'm driving on the way home. I feel a hand on my leg. It's Jonathan getting my attention from the front seat. I thought he was sleeping.

He speaks, "Next time he drives, you sit up front." There is a vein popping out of Jonathan's head that I've never seen before. He must have been awake the entire time. Oh, the horror he must have seen.

I lean back in my chair, and check the security of my seatbelt. Twenty more minutes, how many "Our Fathers" can I do in twenty minutes?

As Holiday Inns go, this one looks pretty good. I'd say it is relatively new, six floors high. The windows are clean, the parking lot is big, with plenty of spaces. The little bit of snow on the ground is carefully plowed to the side, and you can see some of the groundwork and landscaping trying to poke itself out from behind the late autumn white stuff. On the marquee it says, "Have a safe and happy Thanksgiving." Not a bad place. I don't know why we can't stay there.

Down the block is the American Inn. Flip has reserved two rooms here, one for him, and one for Jonathan and me. The American Inn needs a paint job. It's only one floor, but it does have a pool. A pool in Minnesota. What do they do, open it one day out of the year? There are a couple of bushes in front of the main office, and the snow is plowed to the sides, just not very well. The marquee does wish travelers a happy Thanksgiving, but it also advertises hourly rates, and HBO. I really hope Dusty lets us stay with her.

Flip pulls into the parking lot, and slides into a spot next to the office. He literally slides; obviously the parking lot is not nearly as well plowed as I first assumed. We exit the minivan, and go to check in. My first impression of St. Paul: it's cold. From the car to the door is fifteen feet. It takes me ten feet just to breathe correctly. I can see icicles forming on my exhaled breath. Mental note, never come here again.

The office is warm—that's good—but there's an odor. It smells like lamb, or baked feet, or baked lamb feet. The furniture is old, 1960s I'd say. Wooden frames with leather cushions. Red leather cushions. The floor is covered with a bronze, wooly carpet. Or maybe it is an orange carpet that's never been vacuumed. Regardless, I'm sure it holds in the lamb smell real efficiently. There's a coffee pot next to the counter. Either they have hard water problems here, or the coffee pot gets cleaned as often as the carpet. The three of us stare at the coffee pot until we hear the sound of a man at the counter.

"Checking out?" he asks. He's Indian, not American Indian, but India Indian, in his late forties, thick, thick hair, a gray mustache, and he's wearing a bathrobe.

Flip steps forward, "No, we're checking in. Paine; I have two rooms reserved."

The Indian man closes his eyes, takes a deep breath, and walks from behind the counter through a door into the lobby with us. He's not wearing shoes, socks, or slippers. His feet look like he has never worn shoes, socks, or slippers. Yellow nails on toes that point in ten different directions, including backwards. How does one get a toe to point backwards? Each nail is two inches long. He goes over to make some coffee. I look at Flip, and he shrugs. We look at Jonathan, but he is fixated on the toes. The Indian man walks back behind the counter, and the three of us just stare. He points at a sign "Check-in at ten-thirty, you know." And he's gone.

Flip smiles and rubs his hands together, "Who wants some breakfast?"

The omelet bar inside the Holiday Inn was great. A chef with a really tall chef hat makes the omelet in front of you. After our second omelet each, Flip pays the bill, and we drive back to the American Inn. In the car, Jonathan asks the simple question, "Why don't we stay here at the Holiday Inn?"

Flip looks at him, "I called, and they said they were booked." Jonathan turns to me, and we both look at the nearly empty parking lot. "They must have had a few cancellations."

"Flip," Jonathan starts, "I can't stay at the American Inn. That place is a mess. It smells. If you need us to pay for a room, that's cool. No problem, but I can't stay there."

Flip turns to Jonathan, "Hey, that's not it, the Holiday Inn really said they were booked, and I called around. The American Inn is the only place with rooms. I checked Triple A, they rate it four out of five stars. I'm sure the rooms are fine." He smiles.

We slide back into the American Inn parking lot. It's 10:24 am, hopefully they'll let us check in a few minutes early. Once inside, we notice the smell has not dissipated, but now there is an egg aroma on top of it. Add in our six omelets, and the dozen farts from the Holiday Inn to here, and I'm about to puke. Flip hits the bell and this time a lovely Indian woman walks out of the office to behind the counter. She's in her twenties, with big brown eyes, and a light complexion. Her skin is smooth and beautiful. She's wearing blue jeans and a sweater. A tight little sweater that comes right down to her bellybutton. Her hair is long and black, held out of her eyes with a stick/leather type device. "Checking out?"

"No," Flip says with a smile, "We'd like to check in. They have a double, I have a single. The name is Paine, Flip Paine."

"Check in is at ten-thirty, you know." She says and walks away. It's 10:28. Dinner better be good.

Two seconds later, a half a dozen people walk in from nowhere.

They all approach the counter and ring the bell. The woman re-emerges. "Checking out?"

All at once, they say yes.

By 11:15 the last of the check-outs has finished, and Flip is next in line. She asks, "Checking in?"

Flip's smile is gone. "Paine, two rooms."

During the wait, I had a chance to look around the lobby, and sure enough, there was a Triple-A certificate on the wall awarding the American Inn four out of five stars. After further examination, I saw it was dated 1983. I motion to Jonathan and we both chuckle at the ridiculousness of our situation. Flip walks over, "There's a problem."

"Problem, what problem, this is a four star hotel," I say.

Flip really doesn't care. "They only have one room. But it has a kitchenette."

"How many beds?" Jonathan ask.

"Two, queen-sized," Flip says, "and she said she'll bring in a cot at no extra charge." Oh, a cot, great. Flip continues, "She said that this is the last room in St. Paul for the night. All we have to do is go to the room, change and get ready to go to Dusty's. It's already 11:30, we'll leave by three. I'm sure Dusty has room for us where we can crash, and tomorrow when all the rooms are vacant again, I'll set us up at the Holiday Inn."

I want to know how he's going to do that. Reluctantly, Jonathan and I agree. The three of us head outside to get our things and walk to the room, just two doors down from the office.

Room number 3. We swing the door open and step in. Flip first, then me. Jonathan waits outside for the all-clear. He shall wait a few more seconds. Immediately, the one thing that struck me was the bed was unmade. Good thing we waited until 10:30 so they could make the room up. I hesitantly pressed on. It's cold in the room. The heat has apparently been off for at least an hour. Flip was the first one of us brave enough to examine the bathroom. "I think we have to order some towels."

"Why?" I ask. "Are there none?"

"Oh, there are towels in here," Flip replied, "but they are wet and on the floor." We both walk together to examine the kitchenette, which is really a hot plate on top of a small refrigerator. I think the hot plate is washed using the water from the coffee pot in the office.

Jonathan yells from outside, "Is it safe?"

Flip and I both yell back, "No." We walk outside and head straight to the office. As we pass Jonathan he asks us what's wrong, but both Flip and I are pissed. Too pissed to explain what room three is like.

Inside the office, Flip rings the bell and the Indian man walks forward. "Checking in?" "No," Flip calmly states, "we are in room three. Could you send the maid in to clean up? The beds aren't made, and there are no towels in the room."

"Maid's day off, you know," he says. "It is your Thanksgiving. I gave maid day off."

I step forward. "Then who will make up our room?"

"Maid's day off," he repeated. "If you do not want room, you will check out."

The three of us huddle up. I ask Flip if he has any eggs; unfortunately he did not anticipate things moving in this direction, so no. He assures us that Dusty will put us up for the night. Jonathan and I figure something must work out right, so we decide to change our reservation to an hourly stay, get some clean towels, freshen up, then get the hell out of here. Flip walks to the counter. "How about this: you give us some fresh towels, we change our reservation to only two hours—not the night—and by two we check out."

"I cannot do that," the man informs us. "You have already checked in for the night. To re-book the room would be a violation of state law, you know, as it is known to me. But I can give you clean towels."

At this point if we have to pay for the whole night, who cares? Let's just get out of here. We gather our towels and head towards the door. The Indian man stops us. "Here is a bottle of 409 and a can of Comet. If you clean the room, I will remove 25% from your bill, fair?" Flip and I look at this asshole with heavy contempt. Jonathan pushes past us and grabs the cleaning supplies. "Fair."

Back in the room, it's still cold and it's still dirty. Jonathan tells us to give him a few minutes to clean the bathroom, then we can all get ready. Flip and I turn on the TV. There are several parades on and a pre-game show for the Lions game in Detroit. Oh boy, the Lions. On HBO is the making of the movie *The Matrix*. Hopefully they'll show some scenes of Carrie-Anne Moss wrapped in leather. We'll watch this.

Unconsciously, we both back up until the back of our legs hit the edge of the bed. As if in slow motion, I hear Jonathan yell "Noooo!" as Flip and I slowly bend at the knees. I look over to Jonathan and see him reaching out to me and Flip. Suddenly I realize how dire our situation is. I quickly twist my body and place my right hand behind my back, still grasping the remote control I used to turn on the TV. I jab the remote into the bed and push myself forward, avoiding contact with the unmade, unholy, bare mattress. As I look at Flip, he is not so lucky. He has nothing to stop his descent. No leverage, no protection. His eyes light up as he becomes aware of the impending collision of thin blue jeans to bare mattress.

Plop, he's on the bed. Eighteen inches in from the edge of the mattress, his ass has only a layer of denim and cotton between skin and whatever last occupied this room, for an hour. His hands are outstretched, his face grimacing. I am safe standing high above the bed. Jonathan is in denial; if only he had emerged from the bathroom a second earlier.

"Oh man," I say, "that's disgusting." I reach out my hand to help him out.

"You know," Flip says, "It's okay. I've been wearing these pants for twenty-four hours, I'm about to take a shower and clean up. So far, no cold moisture has seeped in." He rolls his eyes as if to verify this last acknowledgement, "Nope, no moisture. It's okay."

Fifteen minutes later, Jonathan is finished with the bathroom, and we all agree Flip should be the first one to clean up.

We are three good-looking men. This place

might be a dump, but we dress it up well. Flip's wearing a black suit with a black Liz Claiborne t-shirt. It's seventeen degrees outside, and he's wearing a t-shirt. Jonathan has on Dockers and a sweater with a tie underneath. I have on gray suit pants, and a red, Christmas-y tie. Santa golfing. So I'm jumping the holiday gun just a bit, but if the stores can put out Christmas displays before Halloween, then I can wear my Santa tie on Thanksgiving.

Jonathan walks over to Flip. "Have you purged?" Purge: a simple, elegant way to say shit. Jonathan's parents were not ones to swear much as he was growing up and saying purge was a unique way to approach a difficult topic. Both of his parents work in computer-related fields where "purge" means dump. Jonathan grew up being told to always purge before long trips, or stressful situations. He's very regular.

"I don't have to go," Flip informs us.

Jonathan puts his hands on Flip's shoulders, turns him, and pushes him towards the bathroom. "Trust me, it's for the best."

Flip reluctantly complies, knowing Jonathan will not let up. After two minutes, Flip yells through the door that nothing is happening. Jonathan, with his arms crossed in front of him, nods to me and tells Flip to wait some more. Sure enough, Jonathan knew exactly what he was talking about. Three clear plops soon came from the bathroom. A small part of me felt a high five was in order, but I did not pursue it.

Flip emerged a few moments later. "You know, I feel better."

Jonathan smiles, "I knew you would. Now we are ready."

Flip walks over to his suitcase and digs out Dusty's present. The box is slightly smaller than his fist. As I recall, he went to Bath and Body Works for a gift. That container looks too small for a bar of soap.

"Flip," I ask, "what's in the box?"

"Oh, nothing big," he assures us, "just a little piece of jewelry."

Jonathan reaches for it and takes the box from Flip's hand. "What kind of jewelry?"

"Small, simple," Flip says. After a long pause, "Nothing big."

Jonathan opens the box. "You bought her an engagement ring."

After another long pause, Flip realizes there was no way out of this,

87

he has to explain to us the contents of the box. "Yes, I bought her an engagement ring. Why else do you think we drove here, why else do you think we are at the American Inn? I spent five grand on this thing, and I intend to use it. Tonight."

Jonathan and I are too shocked to answer. In the back of my head, I thought maybe he would pull something like this, but now that I'm actually confronted with it, I'm completely shocked.

Flip continues, "I would like to think my two best friends would be happy about this. I'm ready to take the next step in my life, and I decided I want to take it with her. I'm not afraid. For eight months I thought about this day. I thought about this girl. Nothing matters to me other than this. Nothing has ever meant more to me than this. I'm a twenty-six year old orphan, my grandparents raised me, and I lost them last year, and until I met Dusty all I thought about was how much life sucked. I know this is crazy, but for eight months, I've been happy. Even when you guys did not want to come, I knew it would work out. I knew we would be here. I know this is the thing to do. This is love, and I've spent too long away from Dusty, and right now she's eight miles down the road. I never want to be even that far from her again."

"Guys, I believe that fate has led me here. Why else would I drag the two of you half way across the country? It's fate." Flip turns to me, "And if anyone knows something about fate it's you, Ulysses. That story about your parents? Hell, they were slated to be with each other a hundred and ten years before they ever met. This is real, and it's what I want."

"Don't make me feel wrong about this, guys. It's all I have, and all I'll ever need."

I step forward, "Jonathan, what do you say we go meet Flip's fiancé?"

Jonathan smiles, "Any girl who marries him, I got to meet." We both pat Flip on the back, and he pulls us in for a hug. Jonathan pulls away slightly, "You know, in a place like this I'm sure there are hidden cameras. Let's not look too gay, after all, we are getting into a purple minivan."

Good point. We separate, and head to the office to pay the bill.

Flip rings the bell, and the Indian woman comes from the office. "Checking in?"

"No," Flip answers, "we changed our reservation to a two hour stay, we are checking out."

"You cannot change reservation, you know, state law," she replied.

"Oh, that's right, I forgot." Flip was trying to save a few bucks. "The other man did say that if we cleaned our room he'd give us 25% off the room, and we cleaned."

"That is the maid's job, no discount," she answered.

"But he said it's the maid's day off. We, he," pointing to Jonathan, as Jonathan places the cleaning supplies on the counter, "cleaned the room."

"It is not the maid's day off," she said, "he is the maid. Bevesh, out here now!" she screams to the back. He enters from the office and she yells at him in some godawful language. If that's Indian, no wonder Columbus went the wrong way to China; I wouldn't want to pass that sound either. The Indian man yells something back and she turns to us. "He was wrong, you pay full price, $65.25. Thank you."

Flip smiles, "That's fine." He reaches into his pocket and pulls out the cash. She gives Flip a receipt, and we head out the door. Flip stops and turns. "I'm sorry, one last thing. I need to stop at a store and grab groceries, is there anything around here?"

"Convenience store down the block," she said with a smile, pointing us in the direction of the store.

Flip thanks her, and wishes her a happy Thanksgiving. Jonathan and I do the same. I wonder how long it takes egg to freeze outside in Minnesota. I think we'll find out soon.

A dozen eggs cost three dollars. Jonathan isn't very sure what Flip was up to until I fill him in, noting the parking lot incident last weekend. To my surprise, Jonathan is okay with what Flip was about to do. As a matter of fact, Jonathan volunteers to assist in the "handling of rage." After all, he was the one who cleaned.

We park the minivan just past the American Inn. Flip and Jonathan go through their bags and grab their sneakers, in case there's a fast getaway. I watch out for cops, and if I find one, I'll have to distract him, flag him down, ask for directions. Jonathan reaches into the egg carton and grabs six. Flip takes one away and says they'll take five each, leaving two. He explains that so far the trip has not gone as planned, so they should prepare for any unexpected turn of events.

It's 2:20 pm; so far we are still good to arrive at Dusty's by three o'clock. Flip and Jonathan exit the minivan. I start looking out for police. In the distance I can actually hear the opening theme from *Mission: Impossible*. Within seconds they arrive at the American Inn. Jonathan starts to wind up when Flip stops him. Flip tells Jonathan this is a stealth operation. Do nothing to draw attention. Flip walks to door number three, and drops an egg six inches above the door knob. Just enough to crack and ooze all over. Jonathan tosses one from inches away that lands in the door jam.

They move to the lobby and office with eight eggs left. Flip insists that they get eggs on the inside, for example the coffee maker, the red leather chair, and the bell. Jonathan is a little nervous about going inside. Jonathan is a good person; this operation is the most evil thing he has ever done.

Flip comforts him, "Listen, they only came out of the office when we rang the bell. We'll place the eggs inside the coffee pot, in the filter, under the chair, on the bell, on the door handle to the lobby from behind the counter, and on the door leading to the outside. The last two we keep for when we're out. If all is clear, we hurl them at the windows, but only if we have an all clear."

Flip and Jonathan enter softly into the lobby. They gently place the eggs in the proposed locations, gently like a mother would for her child's first Easter egg hunt. It is difficult to be stealthy when it comes to cracking eggs, but Flip's a pro. He grabs a rock, and the two delicately crack the eggs and pour the yoke where the most damage can be done. Ninety seconds later, our two heroes emerge from the lobby.

"On three," Flip whispers to Jonathan after verifying the coast is clear. "One. Two. Three." Flip hurls his egg…crash…splat. Egg splatters all over the front window, perfectly covering "A" through "c" of American Inn. Jonathan is not so lucky. As he steps to throw, he hits a patch of ice and slips. Trying to catch himself, he moves his hand to the ground to cushion the fall. Crash…Splat. With egg in hand, he hits the ground, splattering egg all over his right pant leg. Flip erupts in laughter. "You loser."

"Shit," Jonathan screams. "Shit, help me up, I got egg all over me."
As Flip reaches down to help him up, Jonathan looks into the office and
sees someone; the Indian man must have heard the commotion outside
and is coming to investigate. "Oh shit, he came out of the office, shit,
let's go." Flip and Jonathan turn to the road, and make a run for the minivan. After a couple of slips, they get their legs underneath them, and
head out.

Bevesh, looking out the window, heads for the door asking, "Hey,
what is it you are doing out there?" By the time he gets outside, Flip
and Jonathan are well out of sight; a nearly clean getaway. As Bevesh
reaches for the door handle that leads into the office, Flip hears him
scream to the Indian woman inside the office. "Oh, it has happened
again. Why eggs, always eggs."

I'm watching my rearview mirror and I see Flip and Jonathan rac-
ing to the car. I open the side door with the remote button, and put the
car in drive. Flip dives in, followed by Jonathan.

"Operation Egg American was a success," Flip says, "but we have
one casualty. Jonathan fell on an egg."

Jonathan, leaning on his left side, "Ulysses, stop somewhere so I
can clean up, please."

I hit the accelerator, and we are gone.

We are three sad, sad men.

Flip and I stand in the grocery store

for twenty minutes while Jonathan tries to remove egg from Dockers. After a little soap and holding his pants under the hand dryer, he is 90% successful. There was still a little egg odor. I'm sure the turkey will mask it.

By quarter past three, we are heading towards Dusty's. Flip is driving and very quiet. Jonathan is continually touching his pants and then smelling his fingers. He may be only ten percent egg smell now but that's still ten percent more than anyone should be. Flip will not let him change into his jeans; it's not appropriate for Thanksgiving dinner. I'm hungry.

A couple lefts, a couple rights and we are on this handsome, long road, Rose Street. The houses are close together and all very similar, they look like the type built after World War II. This looks like a nice neighborhood. There are several cars along the road, masking all the snow piled to the side. Flip's cruising at about ten miles an hour. He's in a zone, not talking to Jonathan or I at all. He's sweating. We stop on the side of the street opposite two houses. I ask Flip which house, and he's frozen.

"Flip," I tap him on the shoulder. "Are we here?" No answer. The house on the right looks empty, the house on the left seems to have life inside. The chimney is pouring smoke, and several cars line the driveway, and sidewalk. "Flip!"

He hits the gas, and Jonathan and I are pulled into our seats. Jonathan and I try to get his attention, but he's gone. About five blocks down, he slams the brakes. "No way can I do this," Flip tells us. "I haven't talked to her for months, she didn't even give me her address. Why did you guys let me do this? She's going to think I'm a nut! Holy Shit!"

Jonathan looks at me, and then slaps Flip in the back of the head, "You asshole. You dragged us fourteen hundred miles from home on Thanksgiving, just to flip out. Pussy!" Flip looks at him blankly.

I chime in, a bit more subdued, "Flip, you came way too far in terms of adulthood, not to mention driving, to turn back now. What was all that 'I love her, I don't want to be away from her' crap for if you're going to chicken out now?" Flip turns to me blankly.

Jonathan jumps out of the minivan, but before he shuts the door he calls Flip an asshole one more time for good measure. He starts walking back the way we came.

"Flip, pull it together, she's just a girl…a person," I say. "No big deal. Just a person."

He looks to the floor, then back at me. "But Ulysses…"

"No buts, she's only a girl, and whether you like it or not, you are a great guy—a little crazy, but a great guy. She found out in Daytona eight months ago. Let's go remind her." That's the best I can do at inspirational.

"Just a girl, huh?" Flip asks me as I nod yes. "I can talk to a girl. Hell, eight months ago she wanted me bad, but all we did was talk. We talked all night." I can hear the confidence coming back. "I can talk to her no big deal. It doesn't matter if we are in Daytona, St. Paul, or the moon. I can talk to her."

"You sure can. Now let's go get Jonathan and have some dinner." I'm real hungry.

Flip slaps the gear box into reverse, guns the accelerator, and pulls off a flawless one-eighty turn. Jonathan is about two blocks down. Flip catches up to him, passes him, and cuts him off. "J…J…Jesus Chrrrrrist it's cold. UUUUlysess, I wa…wa…walked two blocks waiting for y…y…you to talk some sense into…to Romeo. Next time, ta..talk faster."

Flip pulls up across the street from the aforementioned house with the chimney smoking. It's a modest two story home, with a front porch, enclosed of course, a roof that comes to a high point over the porch, and a couple of snow-laden bushes in front. Flip puts the minivan in park, takes the keys, and we all head out. Jonathan and I follow Flip to the front door. Flip is mumbling under his breath, "She's just a girl, she's just a girl." Jonathan is asking me if he smells like egg.

Standing on the front steps, we can hear the party going on inside. Flip rings the bell. After a few moments, an older woman, maybe about 45, opens the door after tugging and grunting at it once or twice from inside the house. Her hair is done up and she's wearing pearls and an apron decorated with images of cats around her waist. She's wearing a red dress under the cat apron, and slippers. "Hi, can I help you?"

94

I think Flip is taken off guard. He was probably imagining Dusty eagerly awaiting his appearance. I have to shove him in the back with my shoulder to get him to talk

"Hi. Hello. Hi. Happy Thanksgiving. I'm Fred. Paine. Fredrick Paine, Flip. Everyone calls me Flip. I'm a friend of Dusty's. Is she home?" He's so smooth.

The woman answers, "No, Dusty's with Tyson and the boys. Flip, was she expecting you?" Just then an orange cat runs from the hall and bumps Flip in the knee. It is a very big cat. Flip leans down to stop the cat from running out, and the cat jumps into his arms.

"Um, yes ma'am, Dusty and I are friends and we were talking and she said I should maybe come visit her for Thanksgiving. I think this is yours," Flip hands the older woman the cat he just caught. "But I guess she forgot, so I guess we'll be on our way."

I'm starving, and Flip is now so easily sending us on our way. The woman puts her hand out. "No, no. It's Thanksgiving, and I always cook more than I have to. Besides, Tarkenton seems to like you. Dusty's just picking everyone up, you know, she'll be here soon. Come in. Please." What a nice lady. "And who are your friends, Flip?"

"These are my two best friends, Ulysses McHugh and Jonathan Sullivan. We're from Boston," Flip introduces us.

"Boston," the woman says, "Dusty has never been to Boston."

"Oh no, we met in Florida," Flip is quick to answer.

"Oh, pahk the cah in hahvahd yahd…" she says with a smile that we were helpless against. You say you're from Boston, and people think that gives them free reign to make fun of your speech. Well, someone should fill Mrs. Dusty in on the fact that the Revolutionary War started in Boston, therefore the country was first born in Boston, meaning that the language started in Boston, and everyone else is screwing it up, you know? And I have to get to the bottom of this "you know" stuff, can't people around here say "wicked"? Dusty's mother continues, "Well, I'm her mother, and come on in, I'll introduce you to the family. You already met Tarkenton." Dusty's mom introduces us to twelve other people in the house. An assortment of aunts, uncles and cousins. Finally we come to an older man, one I have quickly noticed from the few family photographs hanging around the house featuring him and Dusty's mother. "And this is Dusty's dad, Mr....." He interrupts.

"Call me Buddy, you know. So you boys know my Dusty from Florida. Tell me, is she going to pass this year? I am not paying for any more school, you know." The three of us are dumbfounded.

The mother pipes in, "Now Buddy, these boys don't want to talk about school. Would you boys like a drink? Come with me." We gleefully follow. I don't think we'll ever find out Dusty's last name.

Mrs. Dusty gives us all a cream soda, then excuses herself to the dining room to add three more settings. We have a few minutes to evaluate our current situation. "Who's Tyson and the boys?" Jonathan asks.

Flip looks at me, "I don't know, she said she's from a big family, maybe it's her brother."

"Maybe it's her husband and their kids," Jonathan offers.

"No way," Flip replies.

"Two things," I start. "Where are the appetizers, and why the hell does everyone say 'you know'? It's starting to get to me, you know."

"Will you guys keep it together. I'm nervous enough." Flip wipes some sweat from his brow. "Once Dusty gets here, everything will be cool."

I finally find some cheese and crackers,

and things are looking better. The rest of the "Dustys" seemed okay with our intrusion, although they thought we were still students. But, you know, I'm fine with that, you know. Flip's sweating seemed to slow down, and Jonathan smells less and less like egg. The Cowboys are playing the Buccaneers on TV, and that seems to have all the male attention in the house. The Cowboys need to lose in order to help the Vikings' playoff chances, because the Vikings are only one game ahead of da' Boys for a wildcard spot. All the women in the house are working on the meal. It smells great.

Suddenly, without much notice, the front door opens rather easily, and a beautiful woman walks in the house. She's wearing a long black skirt, with a slit all the way up to the thigh, exposing the boots that come up just under the knee. As she removes her coat, we can see the tight black tank top under a tight see-through shirt. Nice tits. When the coat is completely removed, she shakes the static out of her hair. Long, wavy, brown hair. Jonathan and I turn to Flip, and judging by the sweat and the dropped chin, that's Dusty. Flip unconsciously starts to smile, from ear to ear. He steps forward, passing between Jonathan and me. Dusty is half-turned from Flip, and does not notice his approach. As he steps ever so closer, she removes her gloves, exposing brightly polished red fingernails. Flip's within earshot of her now. You can see him taking in a deep breath as he casually wipes the new sweat from his head. Dusty quickly spins from front to back to open a closet door and hang up her coat. As she reaches forward, a large man takes her coat; this must be her brother. He's about 6 foot 6 inches, very broad in the shoulders; he kind of looks like he could play professional football somewhere. Flip is right behind her now, he's reaching to her, his hand is almost on her waist.

Dusty hands her brother the gloves, leans towards him, and kisses him on the lips, significantly smudging very red lipstick. I am less likely to believe this giant is her brother. Flip catches this as well, freezes, and turns to Jonathan and me. His eyes are as big as volleyballs. Jonathan and I motion to him to get out. If this is Tyson, and Tyson is not her brother, Flip is in harm's way. Flip takes one more look at the back of Dusty, drops his arm, takes two steps backward, and turns around, right into an end table. Dusty hears the commotion and turns from the giant man. "Oh, are you ok?" she asks, having no idea yet who she's talking to.

"Fine," Flip says, not turning, but stepping around the table and heading for Jonathan and me. It vaguely sounds like he is trying to disguise his voice; why would he try to disguise his voice? Just before he makes it to us, Dusty's mom intercepts him from nowhere.

"Oh, Flip," she asks, "Do I hear Dusty, is she here?" She grabs Flip by both shoulders, turns him around, steps in front of him and grabs his hand. "She'll be so excited to see you." She walks him over to the front door. "Dusty."

"Hi Mommy," Dusty says, as a couple more large men walk in the front door.

"Hi honey, happy thanksgiving," Dusty's mom welcomes her. "Look who's here; a friend of yours dropped in." Flip is pulled in front of Dusty and the two lock eyes for the first time in eight months. Clearly, a lot has changed. Jonathan whispers in my ear if we should get our coats. Is he kidding? This could prove to be a lot of fun.

Flip starts, "Hi Dusty, it's me, Flip...." She has no idea who he is. She is staring blankly at him. Dusty gives him a good squint, because we all know squinting helps with memory. She starts to grin, and begins nodding her head as if she honestly does recognize him. Flip continues, "...Flip from Florida. Daytona..." under his breath, barley audible to anyone but her, "...spring break."

Boom. Now she gets it. Flip from spring break. She abruptly grabs his hand and squeezes it, and starts talking in a very abrupt pace. "Flip, from Florida, how are you, it's been a while. I don't think you met my fiancé, Tyson Wheeler, University of Florida, class of '95, you know. Tyson plays with the Vikings, you know. Tyson Wheeler, of the Minnesota Vikings. And these are Tyson's friends, the defensive line of the Vikings—Orlando, Trey, and Ortiz. So, thanks for stopping by, I'll see you back in Florida. Bye bye now."

"Oh, stop that, Dusty," Her mom jumps in. "Flip and his friends are staying for dinner." She introduces Jonathan and I, and we wave. Dusty's mother calls Jonathan Johnny, and one of the Vikings refers to him as John-boy. Neither is corrected. Tyson's friends are much larger than Flip's friends. I think the three of us are sweating quite a bit right now.

Jonathan leans into me, "Do you think we should tell these guys that our minivan is purple because we are fans of the Vikings?" That doesn't seem like a good idea, and Jonathan definitely smells like eggs.

Aside from traveling fourteen hundred miles in one day, canceling the only hotel reservation in the state of Minnesota at the American "Egg" Inn, and learning that not only is Dusty engaged, but engaged to a defensive lineman for the Minnesota Vikings, nonetheless, this has been an okay Thanksgiving. I got to sit next to Orlando Johnson-Harris. He had fifteen sacks last year in San Diego, and when Minnesota picked him up as a free agent, he signed the largest contract ever for a lineman. Oh, and he ate like an animal. I have never before in my life seen a display like that. I let him use my knife. Pretty cool. They made Jonathan sit at the kids table, because he smells like eggs, though that was not the reasoning provided; but we know the truth, he smells like eggs. And Flip sat as far as he could from Dusty, in between her father and another defensive lineman. He stayed quiet throughout dinner. I had his back—whenever someone would try to engage him in conversation, I'd pipe in. It didn't matter what I said, I just made up a story to get the heat off Flip. He wasn't eating a lot.

Things felt a little awkward, but I didn't mind; I was hungry. Dusty's mother decides to start a conversation with me. "So Ulysses, that's an interesting name, where'd you get it?" There are two answers to that question: Ulysses S. Grant, Civil War general who defeated Lee and became the eighteenth US president, or Ulysses from the literary classic Homer's *Odyssey*. I don't think this crowd is up on their Homer, nor do I think they can understand how Ulysses is actually Odysseus, and vice versa. I choose to make it simple.

"My parents," I answer. This answer is never enough.

"Oh no, your name, it's so odd," she states. "I don't think I've ever heard it."

That scares me. When I was a kid, other kids always made fun of my name, and I couldn't understand why. It's just a name, like Michael, or Stephen, or Brian, or Frank. Would a rose by any other name smell as sweet? Oops, I'm getting off track; I should just stick to my Homer.

I remember when I was in third grade it was really bad, this little shit named Tommy Kenny would pick on me unmercifully. He and I were fighting at least once a month after school; of course then a fight was just rolling around on the ground until a teacher or parent could break it up. He never beat me up, and I never beat him up, we would just wrestle each other to the ground, and roll over one another. One time I grabbed him, and by mistake I pulled his head into my mouth. He was knocked out for a minute, and I had the bloody lip. Everyone thought he beat me up, and he was too smug to tell people I knocked him out. He and his family moved after the sixth grade and I never saw him again. Shortly thereafter, kids stopped making fun of my name.

By the time I hit college, it was cool to have a unique name. I knew a girl named Piper, and another named Katerina. I also knew two Xaviers. Two. I may not hear the name Ulysses a hell of a lot more than I hear the name Frank, but I don't think there has ever been a Frank president. Okay, maybe Franklin Pierce and Franklin Delano Roosevelt, but they never went by Frank.

"My parents are Civil War buffs," I inform Dusty's mother. "I have a great-great-great-grandfather and a great-great-uncle who both fought in the Civil War, one for each side. My mother's family was originally from Maryland, and my father's from Boston. They met during a convention in Washington, D.C. years ago, and found out that both families actually had a long history with one another. As a matter of fact, one of my mother's relatives used to live in Boston with one of my father's great-great-grandfathers almost one hundred years ago. My parents both teach history back home."

"Interesting," she said.

"That's fate." Orlando turned to me and stated with his big booming voice. Isn't that what Flip said just a few hours ago? Personally, I've thought a lot about my parents getting together, and on occasion I've used fate as the answer, but I don't buy into the fate thing completely. However, at this time I'm not about to argue with a 300-pound lineman, worth ten million dollars per year. Orlando continues, "My parents were only together two weeks before my dad went to Vietnam. They were married the day before he shipped out, two months later he was killed. Seven months later I was born. A lot had to happen at the right time for me to be born, and it was all fate."

Tyson stands up, points at Orlando and screams, "And why did your momma and daddy get together to make you!"

Orlando rises to his feet, "So I could take the Minnesota Vikings to the promise land, baby!" The other lineman all get up and start doing a little dance/wiggle at the table. Everyone in the house ignited with Viking pride, screaming, cheering and clapping at the notion the Vikings are playoff bound. Jonathan and I half-heartedly join, and through the confusion Flip sneaks up behind me and tells me he and Dusty are going to clean up the kitchen.

"Dude," I say under the cheering, "Don't do anything stupid. Do you see the size of these people?!?"

Flip places his hand on my shoulder and assures me everything will be fine.

Dusty's dad gathers everyone and insists they all rally in the living room to find out the Cowboys–Buccs score.

Jonathan and I are the last to get up and head into the living room. He comes over to me and asks if I'm afraid for my life. I comfort him saying that Flip would do nothing so stupid as to make a Minnesota Viking angry with him.

"I hope you are right," says Jonathan, "because one of those large Minnesota Vikings is coming over here right now."

I turn and there is Tyson Wheeler of the Minnesota Vikings coming over to me. He grabs my shoulder and leads me into the den. Tarkenton is sleeping on the piano, but when he sees Tyson he just runs. This can't be good. The den is full of books and pictures, a place no one would walk into while a game that has playoff implications for the Vikings is on in the other room. I'm a little worried now. He offers me a seat. I sit. I hope the cat's gone for help.

"Ulysses," he says my name with an authority I am frankly quite fearful of, "you seem like a smart man. Are you a smart man?" I nod. "I feel like I can talk to you. Maybe even if I needed some advice, confide in you," he continued.

I'm flattered, I think. Better flattered than flattened. "Thanks Tyson, and you seem like a great guy too…" Tyson stands up in front of me and places his hand on my head.

"When I was in college, I once left a pen on a table in the library. When I went back to get it ten minutes later, some guy was using it. I told him it was my pen, and I wanted it back. He said it was his pen, and I should leave him alone. Now, he has several false teeth in his mouth, because I felt he was lying to me. Turns out after I knocked him to the ground and went to pick him up, I found my pen at his feet. Moral of the story, I don't like when I think I'm being lied to."

I have no idea what to say. In the years to come, I will debate over and over in my head what I should have said, but what came out that day is as followed, "Was it a nice pen, like a Cross pen? I know I'd be upset if I thought someone stole my Cross pen, although I never really had a Cross pen, still they look real nice, I could easily become attached to a nice Cross pen..."

"It was a Bic," Tyson interrupts me. "One question, and I recommend the truth. Have you, egg-boy, or the mute ever had anything to do with my Dusty?"

Oh shit. "No, no way, me...ha. What would she want to do with me? I'm no one. Hell, I ask hookers out on dates and they say no. And egg-boy, um, Jonathan, he smells like that all the time. It's glandular." I am furiously rubbing my rock. In two minutes, if I'm still alive, it'll be worn down to dust particles.

"What about the mute," Tyson asks. I was hoping he'd forget about that.

"Did you see him?" Please believe me... "He's wacky. Who would want anything to do with him?" Please believe me..."Between you and me, I think he's been with men." Please believe me.

There is a long silence, I can feel Tyson getting tense. I don't think he bought it. He reaches his massive hand towards my Santa golfing tie, and wraps his fist into it. I know what's coming next, and all I can think is I don't have dental insurance.

"Why don't I believe you?" he says. With both eyes now closed I can only imagine what he is doing now. How long would it be until I felt that huge fist crush my face? How long would it be until I felt anything again? On a lighter note, I would most likely be the subject of an ESPN story: Viking Lineman Crushes Boston Banker on Route to Superbowl.

"Tyson!" I hear from another room, the yelling gets louder. "Tyson!" I'm released, and I open my eyes. Orlando rushes in to the rescue! "Dallas lost!"

"Yes!" Tyson has forgotten about me, and he and Orlando run to the living room to celebrate with the others. We have got to get out of here.

I find our jackets in a bedroom by the den, and quickly scan around looking for Jonathan and Flip, but trying not to get noticed myself. Jonathan sees me lurking around, and taps me on the shoulder; I almost jump out of my skin. "Where's Flip? We have to get out of here."

"Why, what's wrong? These guys all seem pretty cool. You were right, I was worried about nothing." Jonathan said.

"Tyson Wheeler."

"Of the Minnesota Vikings," Jonathan adds.

"Yes, he just threatened to beat me up, and I think he knows about Flip and Dusty." As I tell Jonathan, all the color in his skin escapes. "Now you go check upstairs, I'll check the kitchen and pantry."

"I'm not going upstairs, alone," Jonathan screams. Thankfully, the living room crowd is still cheering. "We look together." Great, so the defensive line of the Vikings can kill us both at the same time.

Jonathan and I enter the kitchen, and no Flip or Dusty; however, the dishes are still in the sink. "Flip!" we both whisper-yell. "Flip!" After looking around, I turn to Jonathan. "He must be upstairs." Then we both hear a thud, and from under the pantry door oozes a red liquid. "Flip!" We rush to open the pantry, only to find Flip pulling up his pants, and Dusty, while in her bra, trying to pick up a bottle of strawberry jelly that crashed and spilt on the floor. "Flip!"

"Jesus, take a picture you two, can't you see I'm catching up with an old friend?" He thinks he is so cool, having sex with the fiancé of Tyson Wheeler of the Minnesota Vikings in her mother's panty while twenty people are having Thanksgiving dinner.

"Tyson just threatened me, and he knows all about you and Dusty."

Flip's eyes light up when I tell him this. He turns to Dusty. "See you next year at spring break." He jumps out of the pantry, tucks in his shirt, grabs his coat, and we all head to the kitchen door.

"Wait, wait!" I yell. "We can't run out of here like a bat out of Hell, we have to be discreet. Casual."

We casually walk towards the front door, not drawing any unnecessary attention to ourselves. I reach for the door handle and give it a pull. The door is slightly jammed. I yank it hard, so hard that I lose control and slam the door into the wall. This alerts Dusty's mother.

"Boys," she yells and walks over, "you're not leaving, are you?" This got the attention of the crowd.

Jonathan looks at Flip, Flip looks at me, and I look at Jonathan. We got nothing. I look at Dusty's mom. "No, we were just heading out to the car...minivan, to get a dessert we forgot. Out in the minivan."

"Oh, surely you all don't have to go outside, it's so cold," she informs us.

"Flip has the keys, and it's Jonathan's dessert, and um… and I, um, I know where we parked," is all I can think of saying.

A crowd has gathered, with no less than three Vikings to see what we are doing. Tyson Wheeler is one of them. From the side, behind a lamp, Dusty's father yells over to Flip, "Hey, XYZ fellow, examine your zipper, you know."

At the same time, Dusty walks out of the kitchen. Her red lipstick is considerably duller. "Has anyone seen my purse? What are you guys are still doing here?"

Tyson looks over to her, and notices right away the lack of lipstick. Add to that we all know Flip's fly is half down, and we all know we are screwed. The three of us, with our backs to the wall know that this might be it. Sure, we can make a dash out the door and to the minivan, but will we be able to beat professional football players in a sprint across the street? Suddenly, as if sent by the Dallas Cowboys themselves, Tarkenton comes over to Flip and then, almost like we are all reading from the same playbook, Flip picks up Tarkenton, Jonathan and I move to the door, and Flip tosses the cat right at Tyson Wheeler, who heroically catches the cat. Bite his nose off, Tarkenton!

The distraction was enough. We fling open the unjammed door and run for the minivan, slamming the door behind us. Please jam again. Flip fishes through his coat pocket for the keys as we run down the stairs. Were cars coming down the street? We didn't have time to look. Flip grabs the remote, and clicks the "lock" button. It's the other one, you idiot. The Minnesota Vikings are hot on our tail, getting through the not-very-jammed door and jumping down the front steps. Jonathan and I run around the front of the minivan, and yell to Flip to open the side door. I hit a patch of snow and ice, and both Jonathan and I slide down the driveway of the neighbor across the street. Flip's in the minivan, yelling at us to stop fooling around. I think Jonathan is screaming for his life right now. Tyson Wheeler crosses the street and starts banging on the driver's side door. Jonathan and I regain our footing and leap for the minivan side door, just as Orlando Johnson-Harris slides on a patch of snow and ice. "We're in, drive. Drive!" Jonathan and I scream as we close the door in tandem.

Flip has locked the doors, and is flipping off Tyson Wheeler, and miming to him what he and Dusty did in the pantry. Tyson Wheeler is not happy with this. He grabs the driver's side rearview mirror, and pulls it off the car door.

"Okay, we're leaving now." Flip floors it as Tyson Wheeler punches our minivan and throws the mirror after us. It's clear why he plays defensive line, he missed us big time with the throw.

Jonathan and I lie in the backseat, catching our breath as Flip turned to us. "That was a nice dinner."

Following that eventful meal, we all agree an

after-dinner drink is called for; actually required. About ten miles down the road we come across a very T.G.I. Friday's-looking place, VanGustaf's Sports Bar. There was no way Tyson Wheeler and the defensive line of the Minnesota Vikings are after us. And if they are, what are the odds they would come here? Regardless, we park the minivan very discreetly, hiding the missing driver's side mirror from the road.

For eight o'clock on Thanksgiving night, VanGustaf's was busy. The bar's locked in the middle of the place and tables with checkered tablecloths scattered around it. Photos hung on every inch of the wall. There was a wall for the Twins, the Timberwolves, the old Northstars, and of course, the Vikings. The picture of Tyson Wheeler had him standing over Emmit Smith, with his Vikings helmet in one hand, the other pointing at a slaughtered Smith. Blood was running down the side of Emmitt's face, along his nose. I wonder if Tyson was penalized for that. We sit on the other side of the bar at a little round table next to a picture of Kent Hrbek holding the '91 World Series Trophy. So that's what it looks like. Jonathan walks to the rest room with a pair of jeans in an effort to get rid of the egg smell.

All the stools around the bar are full, and about half the tables have people. Everyone looks cold.

The ride here was very quiet. I think we were all feeling how close we came to mortality. I don't think I have ever been so scared in my life. Once, back when I was in high school, I was mugged by a couple of guys in Boston. It wasn't too scary; I don't think they were very good at mugging. Maybe I was their first. All they asked for was my wallet, not my watch or the gold necklace that happened to be hanging out over my shirt. Suckers, all they got was five bucks, an old condom, and a picture of Dany I stole from Jonathan. As I mentioned, I was in high school.

While Jonathan is in the men's room, Flip braves the bar and buys us the first round. I have news for him, after tonight's episode, he's buying every round until I'm home. When he makes it back with three Rolling Rocks, I have to ask, "What were you thinking?" With the biggest shit-eating grin I'd ever seen, he recaps the events for me.

"Man, she kept eyeing me all dinner long, and not that 'what are you doing here' eyeing, no it was more like 'I'm going to rip your clothes off' eyeing. When you caused that little distraction and got those muscle-headed idiots all cheering for the Vikings—thank you by the way—she passed me a note. It only had two words: 'Vikings fan?' I shook my head no, and then she suggested to her mom that we clean up the dishes. I didn't even get the chance to ask her about Wheeler, she just pushed me against the counter and started making out with me. I heard the cheering outside, so I just lifted her into the pantry. Ten seconds later, my pants were at my ankles, and her skirt was around her waist. By the way, excellent naked body. Anyway, like any good rodeo cowboy, I lasted my eight seconds, and we were done."

I manage to lift my jaw off the ground to ask the all important question, "Why?"

"It's like the moth to the flame; she just could not resist me," Flip is beaming with arrogance.

"You do understand once a month I wipe the dead moths from my kitchen light just because they couldn't resist that either," I can't resist saying.

"I asked her the same question," Flip replies a bit more humble. "It turns out they were dating back during spring break; as a matter of fact, for about two years. That's why she wouldn't sleep with me, she's moral; well, that was at least until she found out about a stripper in Tampa a couple of weeks ago. The timing was perfect, I was revenge sex." Flip hoists his arms in the air as if he just threw the game-winning touchdown in the Superbowl.

I ask if he was okay with that.

"Sure, we got a free Thanksgiving meal, traveled to a part of the country we've never seen, met some nice people, not to mention a few sports celebrities. And the engagement ring I bought appraised for more than I bought it for, so that will cover all expenses."

My spin on things is a little different. "We were almost killed by very large men, the potatoes were dry, Jonathan smells like egg, and at last count, only one of us had sex, and it wasn't me. Oh, and in case you forgot, we have no place to stay tonight."

"There are plenty of hotels and motels on the highway. We'll find someplace, don't worry." When Flip gets sex, he becomes very confident. That would be comforting if he wasn't such a nut.

Jonathan finally emerges from the men's room at about the time

110

Flip gets the two of us a second beer. He says the egg seeped to his underwear, and he is still having odor problems due to that fact. He tried to wash it out, but this place does not have hand driers, so he sat in a stall with paper towels trying to dab out the moisture. "Do I still smell?" he asks; both Flip and I say no, knowing full well he does still stink, but now it's more eggs and hand lotion than just eggs.

Flip informs Jonathan about how he and Dusty made the most out of the kitchen, and to my surprise Jonathan is excited about Flip's good fortune. His reasoning—at least he got laid.

By ten o'clock, VanGustaf's is packed. The music is blasting from the speakers overhead, the bar is two people deep, and all the tables are loaded. Talking amongst ourselves, we decide that this trip is not the worst experience any one of us ever had. Nor is it anywhere near the most embarrassing. So a wager kicked off and the winner had to buy the next round. We figure that if you win this bet, buying a round of drinks is not a big deal. The ground rules were simple. It has to be an event or an experience where we brought embarrassment upon ourselves, not anyone else. Also, it has to be something no one else ever heard about. Totally new. I picture in my head that in a different life we would be doing this same thing at the local hairdresser, under those huge hair dryers.

Jonathan goes first. "Besides smelling like eggs all day, remember about two years ago I was going to church a lot, twice a week for about six months? Well, it wasn't for the reason I told you guys."

Flip pipes in, "You said you needed to get confirmed before the wedding and you were going to night classes."

"Yeah, and I kept asking why you had to get confirmed if you were getting married in the Protestant church." Flip, Jonathan and I all took doctrine classes together on Saturdays, but for one reason or another, not one of us ever finished.

"Here's the story." Jonathan chugs the last of his beer, and states, "Dany and I had been fighting. To the point I thought the engagement was over. So one night, over my parents' house—they were out of town on vacation—I made her this big candlelight dinner. Everything she liked I had: bagel bites, teriyaki beef from Moy's, homemade cherry cheesecake, and caffeine free Diet Coke. I had her favorite flowers, I had her favorite music playing, everything was perfect.

"The night started off smooth, no arguing, until I reminded her about the time we fooled around on my parent's kitchen floor. Well, it seemed she didn't remember that particular encounter. We fought for an hour, about the kitchen floor, how she said she would never do anything on a kitchen floor. We fought about you Flip, how you look at her weird sometimes. I told her you look at everyone that way once in a while. I yelled at her for cutting her hair, she yelled at me for the Patriots losing Curtis Martin to the Jets. Eventually, I kicked her out of the house. I told her I never wanted to see her again. She told me that was fine with her, and that she was going over your house, Ulysses, and she was going to sleep with you on your kitchen floor to spite me. I told her I thought you might be gay, and wished her luck."

"Thanks," I say to Jonathan in shock as I chug my remaining beer. What would I have done if Dany came to my door looking for a cheap, nothing encounter? Would I jeopardize my friendship, and say what the hell? And on the kitchen floor...I never wash my kitchen floor. Tough call.

"Anyway, if I can finish, she left. Turns out she went over her friend Julie's, and stayed the night, crying. I finished the bottle of wine, and around midnight, drunk as a skunk, I decided to break up with her. I got in my car—by the way, that was a stupid thing to do, I was lucky I didn't kill anyone, especially myself—and I drove to her house. Well, it was dark. I pull in front of the house, get out, stand under her window, pull down my pants, and in the snow I made an "I" and a "U". Then I squat in between the two letters figuring I'll take a dump. I dump U. Poetic."

"After trying for about a minute, I guess the alcohol, the cold, and the fact we never ate got to me, and I passed out. Keep in mind that my pants are at my ankles, I peed on either side of myself, and I had a turtle-head brewing. The next thing I remember I was waking up in Reverend Rivers' basement shower. I had gone to the wrong house; the reverend lives next door. He threatened to call the police and have me arrested. I did the only thing I could. I begged him for mercy, and asked him for spiritual guidance. After I cleaned up my mess, he agreed to probation. I would go to his church twice a week, once for service, once for private lecture. If I show I've grown, he would forget the matter ever happened, considering I never do anything like that again. It was a pretty safe bet I had shit on my last lawn."

"After six months, he told me I was free of my obligation. Dany never found out. I trust she never will."

Flip and I cannot stop laughing. Jonathan is the good one; he never caused any trouble, ever. And to get caught for what he did, by a reverend, is priceless. Flip insist I go next, but there is no way I can top shitting on a holy lawn.

"My story actually has a happy, inspirational ending," I start.

"No," Flip jumps in. "I don't want to be inspired, or feel good afterwards. I want to laugh at you. This ain't a Lifetime movie, no sappiness."

I assure him my story is not a Lifetime movie. "You guys know I did a lot of acting in college, but none in high school? Well, one of the reasons I got into acting in college was because there were a lot of cute girls in the acting classes, and it sounded like fun and it was a way to break out of my shell. I was encouraged to try out for *Romeo and Juliet*. It was going to be the first play in the school's new multi-million dollar auditorium. I had two lines, 'which way ran he who killed Mercutio? Tybalt, that murder'r, which way ran he.' They came after a big fight scene. Well, the day of the opening was big. All the founders and trustees were in town for the dedication. That morning they had a commencement ceremony with the seniors, and a local news cast was going to do a story for the news that night. Needless to say, there was a lot going on that day.

"At 8:15, the curtain went up and everything was going great, with the exception of a piece of the set breaking off during an early fight sequence. One of the actors hit a window frame, it popped off, hitting a stage hand in the back, and you could hear this kid scream 'shit' all the way to the back of the theatre.

"Well, for every show they say there is always one screw up, so I figured we're good. Beginning of act four, after intermission I'm ready to go out. I was wicked nervous, but I had a ton of energy. I hear my cue, and race from behind the wings. I run to my mark, and hit the brakes to deliver my lines. Before I knew what was happening, I was sliding on my back, heading for the lap of the college president.

"A little background—the stage was dusty—sorry, Flip. It was dirty from all the previous activity, and no one swept it up. I was wearing a kilt, and holding a long staff. During my slide all I could think about was my kilt flying up over my head, but I couldn't grab it because I didn't want to lose my staff. I ended up at the feet of the president. He leaned over, helped me up, turned me to the stage, and pushed me up the stairs. I had no idea what to do. There were twenty people on stage, all in shock. There were a thousand people in the seats equally in shock. So, I delivered my lines, and the place exploded. It took a good five minutes before the last chuckle died down.

"I was black-listed for the rest of the year, allowed to work only spotlights and take tickets."

Flip and Jonathan are silent. Flip leans toward me, "That's it? C'mon, at least Jonathan shit on someone, all you did was slip. And if you ask me, *Romeo and Juliet* is rather dull; you gave it a favor by injecting some life into the show."

"Wait a minute," Jonathan turns to Flip, "I did not shit on someone, but on something." Then Jonathan turned to me, "What's the inspirational ending?"

I almost forgot. "The director of the show was the head of the theater department, and he also teaches several classes, including basic acting. He uses my fall as a lesson in his class. But, the way he tells it, after I fall and get up, I turn to the college president, and in character say 'pardon me but yonder step is a bitch.'" The first thing you are taught when you act is that a character in a play is not you. You can draw from yourself, and make relations between you and your character, but no matter what, you must always remember, it is not you, it is a character. Always stay in character." Flip and Jonathan do not seem to appreciate this aspect of acting. Then again, I work at a bank, maybe I'm not really that good of an actor.

"Sorry Ulysses," Flip says, "I have to go with Jonathan's shit story."

I'm not that broken up about it.

"Okay, my turn." Flip rubs his hands together, and leans back in his chair. "Amy Pepperidge. I went out with her for about three months after college. She was really preppy. You know all those yellow polo shirts I clean my car with? She gave them to me. So for her birthday, I bought her tickets for U2 at Foxboro Stadium."

Jonathan jumps in, "Wait, I remember this, she broke up with you that night. You listed it as reason number seventeen why you hate Foxboro Stadium."

Flip holds up his hand, "May I continue? Thank you. Yes, it is

114

well-documented why I hated Foxboro Stadium. And along with the aforementioned reason, and other reasons, such as reason number one, the parking, reason number five, the cold aluminum seats, reason number seven, the bearded woman who refused to serve me beer because my fake ID was technically expired, and reason number thirteen, the Patriots mascot hates me and mocks me, there are two reasons no one has ever heard. Reason 15 and 16, the concealed reasons. Tonight boys, full disclosure."

"So, I buy Amy tickets for U2; I bought four tickets, me, her, and this couple she's friendly with, Ken and Barbie or something. Before the show, we go to this Mexican restaurant. I get a burrito. Bad idea. The mile walk from the parking lot to the stadium packed my bowels, and started a push I quickly became very uncomfortable with. Now, reason number two is I hate the bathrooms inside Foxboro. As a matter of fact, I've often resolved to never use those bathrooms. Well, on this night nature came calling.

"Just before the show, I'm sitting on the cold aluminum seat, and my stomach is turning ten different directions. I was about to shit myself."

Jonathan jumps in, "I bet you wish you had purged."

Flip pauses, looks at Jonathan, throws a grin in his direction, then continues. "So I get up, and head for the bathroom. It's so bad that not only am I going to use a Foxboro Stadium restroom, but I'm going to shit there. Apparently, a lot of other people had the same idea, men and women. Reason number fifteen why I hate Foxboro Stadium: they let women use the men's restroom. Whether on purpose or security just looks the other way, woman were in line in the bathroom. And they were cutting. There was nothing we, and by we I mean men, could do. They came in teams of four or more. The lone man was helpless. One woman would get into the stall, and then allow her friends to sneak in after, or in some cases, with her."

"Well, I'm about to blow the back of my ass off, so eventually, I bump this one girl, who was cutting, and I get into the stall. She bangs on the door a little, but it didn't matter. I barely had enough time to lay paper down on the seat. I think I dropped five pounds of shit into the toilet. I had three courtesy flushes. I couldn't stand the smell myself.

"So, after about ten minutes, I felt the deluge was over and I started to compose myself. Got up, wiped, pulled up my pants, and try to shake out the pins and needles I was feeling from sitting. As I opened the stall, the girl I bumped is standing outside, with a security guard, and she's yelling at me. Then I hear someone comment about the smell that hit when I opened the door, and finally, I noticed Amy was in line with Barbie, or whatever her name was. None of this sat well with me, and I kind of shit my pants."

"Wait," Jonathan throws his arms up. "I would have said something if I could stop laughing. "You just shit for ten minutes, and you still had enough shit inside you that you could not control. Loser."

Flip smiled, "So reason number sixteen is the lack of impartial security at Foxboro Stadium. He never questioned that she was in the men's restroom. Or that she tried to cut me. He just kicked me out, I never got to see the show, I had just shit in my pants, and had no ride home because Ken, or whatever his name was, drove. I ended up ducking in some bushes, taking off my underwear and throwing them away in those bushes. Then I tied my polo shirt around my waist and I had to call my grandparents to come get me. They never asked me what happened, they just brought me clean underpants, and took me home. For some reason, Amy never returned my phone calls."

I interject, "Her loss."

So we have two shit stories, and one slip story. Well, clearly, mine was the least impressive, so it's down to Flip and Jonathan. Although Jonathan's did involve the sacrifice of six good months he'll never see again, Flip has the edge of buying tickets to a show he never got to see. They both took a shit when it came to a girl, but Flip's girl actually saw it, and for this reason, Flip wins the honor of buying another round. Which really doesn't matter because no matter who won, he was buying.

It's getting late, and we still have no place to sleep. We decide that we'll have one last beer. For the record, we only had five over three hours. Actually, Jonathan had four after being delayed in the bathroom. The hint of egg still surrounds him. Flip's buying.

Jonathan and I watch as Flip walks to the bar, and excuses himself between two ladies who were obviously in a conversation, but clearly without male companions. He gives his order to the bartender and takes one step back, allowing the conversation that he had interrupted to resume. He's such a lady killer; not four hours removed from his relationship with Dusty and he's already laying down the ground work for future frustrations. The bartender returns with three Rolling Rocks, Flip leans in again, lays down the money and picks up our beers. As he gets ready to walk away, he stops, turns, and says something to the two women. Jonathan and I can see them snicker as Flip turns around and heads back to our table.

"What did you say?" both Jonathan and I ask at the same time.

Flip places our beers down in front of us and smiles. "I told them that if they wanted to do themselves a favor, they could buy us our next round of beer."

"Flip!" Jonathan was mad, "I'm not drinking any more beer after this. I'm tired and I want to leave."

"Jonathan," I comfort him, "look who you are talking to, do you really think that'll work? You'll be in a bed within an hour." I turn to Flip. "Nice line, did you think of that yourself?"

Flip answers by saying it's part of his stable of pickup lines. I ask if they ever work, knowing full well what the answer is.

"Well," Flip informed me, "I'm hoping to raise my average above the Mendoza line with a few hits back to back."

Jonathan raises his bottle, "Gentleman, a toast to the unimpeachable spirit of one Fredrick L. Paine, a man that knows not of 'no,' only 'next.' And with a clatter of green glasses, we toast our bottle-of-beer-is-half-full friend.

Suddenly, we hear applause and cheering from the bar; surely everyone else did not join us in our toast. "I wonder what that's all about," I ask, as if Jonathan or Flip could answer.

"We're in Minnesota," Flip answered. "They do strange things to keep warm, you know."

"Maybe random group cheering is one of those warmth retention techniques," Jonathan adds.

Then we hear a voice looming large over the crowd. After a few seconds, everyone settles down; it's like a political rally. Who is this, Jesse Ventura? From our vantage point, all we can see are the backs of everyone's heads.

Finally, it is quiet enough for the voice to be heard. "Ladies and gentlemen," the voice starts. It's a big voice, one with resonance and thrust. The crowd is captivated. "My friends and I are hoping you can help us."

Someone from the crowd interrupts, "Anything for you, baby." And the crowd goes crazy.

The three of us stand up and try to see who's talking, but we can't get any kind of view. It's like a Red Sox game; you could be sitting behind a pillar the whole game, and until the action moves, you only get the sounds of the game. Who is this? The crowd settles again.

The voice starts up again. "We are looking for three friends of ours in town today, from Boston."

Three friends from Boston? We are three people from Boston. This might turn out bad; it couldn't be Tyson Wheeler with the defensive line of the Minnesota Vikings addressing the crowd, could it? The three of us huddle up. "What do you think?" Jonathan asks. If Tyson Wheeler of the Minnesota Vikings did indeed track us down here, then we have serious trouble.

"I think the odds are good we are about to get our asses kicked," I say. What's the plural of ass? Is it asses? Maybe I should have said butts? "Let's get the hell out of here. Flip?"

"You think I'm going to argue?"

There's another cheer from the crowd. Someone from the crowd yells out the name Tyson, and with that the three of us get all the confirmation we need. We are leaving!

There are only two exits, the front, which is the center of attention, and a fire exit in the back. The rock is out of my pocket, and I'm rubbing it with both hands. Jonathan sees this, figures it can't hurt, and helps me rub.

Undoubtedly, the fire exit is alarmed, so that is no option. With any

118

luck, if we lay low, no one will recognize us, and we can casually exit once Tyson Wheeler of the Minnesota Vikings has moved away from the front.

Tyson is heard over the crowd again, "These three guys are Cowboy fans," a lie, "and we want to welcome them the Vikings country. One's tall and has a stupid name like Ulysses or shit-head, or something, another is chubby and smells like eggs, and the third is a real ladies man, just stupid as dirt."

We are so dead. And this isn't "we are in trouble" dead, we are *dead*. If we don't get out of here, my parents die grandchild-less. "What are we going to do?" I ask from the back of the bar, squatting down with the chubby and the stupid one.

"I say we split up." Flip figures, "These guys are looking for three of us, not one. We all head for the minivan separately once the Vikings start looking for us."

"Ok," I agree. "We'll hang back here, and once the crowd moves with Tyson, we sneak out." In the long history of escape plans, this might be the least thought out.

"Hey," a whisper from the back calls out to us. It's one of the women Flip was hitting on. "Are you those three guys?" she asks.

"No," I say.

"No!" Jonathan confirms.

"I'm any guy you want me to be," Flip offers with a wink and nod. We both hit him hard across the head.

She motions Flip over with her finger. Both Jonathan and I try to stop him, but we can't. He's determined to find out what she wants. She leans over to Flip, cups her hand to whisper something in his ear, and screams, "I hate the Cowboys!" Then she gets up and screams over to Tyson with her arms in the air, "Tyson baby, they're over here, sweet thing!"

"Holy shit!" Jonathan and I make a run for the front door, while Flip heads for the emergency exit. The whole bar is focused on Flip, Tyson Wheeler and the defensive line of the Minnesota Vikings head through the crowd. Everyone shifts to Flip's position. The door is free. No one is guarding the front door. Jonathan and I can get out and call the cops. We can only hope Flip can survive until our return.

At the door, we turn back to the emergency exit. Flip throws it open only to find a large man guarding that door. To my surprise there was no alarm. Flip tries to go through him, but the large man stops Flip in his tracks. If Emmit Smith has problems with these guys, what chance does Flip have? I grab Jonathan's arm, "We'll come back for him, let's get some help." I push the door open, and standing in the entrance is Orlando Johnson-Harris and two other large men. Orlando has a brace around his leg and crutches. Jonathan and I stop dead in our tracks.

"Johnny, Ulysses. Nice to see you again. Little something about football, sometimes the running back gets through the defensive line," Orlando informs us pointing to himself. "That's why we have linebackers," as he motions to his two large friends. They step forward and grab Jonathan and I.

The two of us are rushed back into the bar where we are reunited with Flip. There's that scene in *Return of the Jedi*, after Leia has freed Han from Jabba, and Luke has killed the monster in the pit using a bone and a gate. Our heroes are reunited, quite like the three of us, and Han asks, "How's it going?" And Luke answers, "Same as usual," and Han replies, "That bad, huh." Right now I wish things were that good for the three of us.

The crowd at the bar cheers as we are herded together. I don't think these people know the weight of our situation. Flip just stares at Tyson Wheeler. Jonathan looks as if he's praying, and I'm looking around, there must be someone in the bar who will stop this.

From within the crowd someone screams, "Kill the Cowboy-loving sons of bitches." This sends everyone into an uproar. Flip is still staring straight at Tyson Wheeler. I don't think Tyson Wheeler of the Minnesota Vikings is going to be intimidated by a guy named Flip who works at North Union Bank. Tyson steps towards Flip and speaks in a normal voice, but with the crowd so crazy, only Flip can really hear him. I think I catch the word "Kill," a few times, but I might be mistaken. If only I could somehow let these people know we have a purple minivan in honor of the Vikings.

Flip, still intensely staring at Tyson, leans towards him and starts talking in his ear, very calm, very collected. Tyson then motions to the man holding Flip to release him, and subsequently, Flip is released, and pushed over to Jonathan and I, and we are released. But not let go.

"What did you say to him?" I asked.

Flip got close to Jonathan and I and filled us in on his and Tyson's intimate conversation. "He told me that he was going to rip my dick off and kill me with it. So I called him a pussy, and asked why he's never been to a pro-bowl. Then I asked him if he ever heard Dusty try to hold back a scream of passion, like she had to with me."

"Are you crazy?" Jonathan grabs him. "He's going to kill you."

"I have a plan," Flip tells Jonathan and me. For some reason, I'm not comforted. "When you see me give the signal, do whatever you have to do to get through those doors."

"That doesn't sound like a plan," I quietly stress. "That sounds like what we just did, and got caught doing."

Flip snapped, "Will you trust me! Jesus Christ, I need you two to trust me right now. Just get through that door."

"What are you going to do?" I ask.

"I'm going to fight him," Flip said confidently as he turns, and walks over to Tyson Wheeler, the very large defensive lineman of the Minnesota Vikings. "Pro-bowl-less pussy, are you ready?" Flip calls out over the crowd noise.

The crowd fills with "Oooh's" after the comment. They know Flip has no chance. One punch, and he's folding like the Vikings in the playoffs. Sorry, but it's true.

Flip continues, "You know, after I'm done here with you..." he leans closer to Tyson, "...I'm going back over to Dusty's and I'm going to give it to her again."

I can actually see the fire in Tyson's eyes. This is totally ridiculous, Flip is maybe five foot ten and weighs no more than one hundred and eighty-five pounds. Tyson is a monster, six foot six, and well over three hundred pounds. He'll kill Flip and Flip is totally instigating him. Tyson pushes Flip in the chest, and sends him flying towards the bar.

"You know the old saying, 'The bigger they come'?" Flip asks Tyson as he gets off the bar.

"Don't even bother with that shit, dumbass," Tyson asserts.

"I was talking about me." Flip lunges forward and pushes Tyson as hard as he can. Judging from Flip's reaction Tyson flew back twenty feet, but in reality, maybe an inch or two. Tyson is a rock and barely acknowledges Flip's advance. "Dusty said I was twice as big as you are."

That, on the other hand, gets a reaction. Tyson literally throws Flip to the ground and then starts to remove his jacket, presumably to finish the job without getting blood on suede.

Flip's verbal bantering, plus the way Tyson just pushed him with so much force is a farce. The rest of the Minnesota Vikings are laughing. Hell, they are practically on their backs in hysterics. Flip pulls himself up and tries to regain his composure at the bar. He fixes his shirt and walks back to Tyson Wheeler.

"Dusty pushed me up against the kitchen counter harder than that."

"That's it, asshole," Tyson states as Flip gets right in his face. "I'm sending you home in a hearse." Tyson clenches his fist and pulls his arm back, ready to strike.

In my lifetime, I've seen many amazing feats: The Red Sox blow game six of the '86 world series; Larry Bird steals an inbound pass against the Pistons and feeds DJ for the win; the Florida re-count; and Dany's breasts. Well, actually it was only one, she bent over to clear a seat for me one day over her house while wearing a v-neck t-shirt and no bra. For half a second I saw all the way down to her belly-button. It was awesome, but of course we were only seventeen. I know I hit puberty years earlier, but that was the exact moment it kicked in.

So anyway, Tyson's fist is clenched and in the ready position. Flip has his shoulders back, staring Tyson right in the eyes. Suddenly, Flip breaks his stare and looks down between Tyson's feet, says something and points to the floor. Tyson, momentarily, is taken off guard by this and looks down. Flip then, without hesitation, nails Tyson in the gut. Tyson crouches slightly over, releasing his fist and dropping both arms to his gut. The crowd is silent. Flip then reloads, and hits Tyson square in the nose. When his head shoots back, blood is evident. The only sound you can hear in the bar is that of Flip's fist connecting with Tyson's nose, CRACK. In all the years I have known Flip, he's never been very accurate. Sports like tennis or even darts are not his specialty; they require too much concentration and aim. Well, for what it's worth, Flip's aim has improved one hundred-fold. It was like Tyson's nose was three feet wide, and Flip put everything he could into that punch, his feet actually left the ground. Finally, with Tyson arched back, Flip takes a half step back, and with his right leg plants his foot perfectly between Tyson's massive legs, actually lifting him ever so slightly off the ground. As Tyson lurches forward to protect his nuts, be it too late, Flip grabs Tyson's head, and pulls it down to his left knee.

With a giant thud, David has slain Goliath again. No longer is this a sports bar, now it's more of a greenhouse, with a hundred patrons doing their best impersonation of a Venus flytrap. Flip stands over Tyson, and with one arm curled across his chest, and the other pointing at Tyson's broken body Flip proclaims, "I'm the mayor of kick-ass city, and you just became a taxpayer, you prick. Don't ever cheat on Dusty again!" The rest of the Vikings are in shock. They have yet to react. How can they react? This is the New York Jets beating the Baltimore Colts in Superbowl III. This is the Patriots beating the greatest show on turf in Superbowl XXXVI. This is impossible. Flip quickly kneels in front of the broken Tyson Wheeler, "Who's the dumbass?"

The shock is starting to wear off, and the rest of the Vikings will figure out what has happened. Flip jumps up and turns to Jonathan and I. "That was the signal!" We shake off our amazement and turn for the door. Orlando is there with one of his linebacker friends. Neither one of them can fathom what they just saw. I have enough time to quickly kick Orlando's crutch from underneath his arm, and send him flying into his friend. As Orlando drops, Jonathan grabs the other crutch, and throws open the door. He runs out, with Flip and I right behind him. As we look into the parking lot, there is nothing but one hundred feet of cold air between us and the minivan.

We could hear the crowd inside finally realize what just had happened. Jonathan props the crutch under the door handle, and the three of us run for our lives. Flip hits the door remote, and we are safely inside the car. Huffing and puffing, Jonathan and I are in utter amazement. "What did you say to him?" I asked.

Flip smiled as he reached for the glove box, "I asked him if he dropped his wallet."

"That's it?" Jonathan says shocked.

"I'm surprised it worked, too." Flip grabs the last two eggs from the dozen, and jumps in the back. "Ulysses, drive, I'll man the guns. C'mon kids, we're not out of this one yet!" I jump into the driver's seat, and Flip swings open the side door. I slam it in reverse, and spin the minivan backward. I pull into drive, and stomp the accelerator just as the crowd inside the bar force the door open. Flip hurls two eggs into the crowd, as we speed off into the night. Jonathan screams in the background, "The name is Jonathan, asshole!"

With time, the legend of this episode will undoubtedly grow, and for future generations Flip, Jonathan, and I all agreed that the only way to end the story was to have one egg hit Tyson Wheeler of the Minnesota Vikings, and the other to hit the girl at the bar who ratted us out.

Harry Houdini had a tank of milk. Frank

Morris had Alcatraz. Steve McQueen had a German POW camp. All great escape artists in their own right. Add Ulysses McHugh, Fredrick (Flip) Paine, and Jonathan Sullivan to that list—we had Minnesota. It was a hundred to one that any of us would get out of that bar without a scratch, and for all three of us to do it was simply a miracle. Flip temporarily became a ninja. He laid out that football player in seconds. Boom, boom, boom, bam. It was over. And then to have enough left to egg them as we sped away. Well, I'm not ashamed to say this, but Flip is my new superhero. Call the Justice League and admit Flip. This status should last at least until sunrise.

We're cruising east along Interstate 94. I'm driving and Flip and Jonathan are in the back, watching the headlights behind us to make sure we are not being followed. Jonathan wants to dump the car and pick up a new one; I remind him that we aren't Bonnie and Clyde. Even if we were, either him or Flip would have to be Bonnie. I'm not a Bonnie, I'm a Clyde.

The time is approaching midnight, and the three of us are exhausted. Since yesterday morning we've traveled fourteen hundred miles, had a huge turkey dinner, several beers, and beat up half the Minnesota Vikings defensive line, all on very little sleep. A sign on the road says there is lodging at the next exit. We take the turnoff and there, shining in the distance, is a big, beautiful, glowing homage to the America traveler. Holiday Inn.

"What do you mean you have no vacancies?" Flip asks a very tired hotel clerk.

"I'm sorry sir, we're booked solid tonight. Can I help you with anything else?" Oh, yeah, since we can't have a room, where can we get a good pedicure? What does he mean help us with anything else? It's an inn, all we want are rooms.

Flip turns to Jonathan and I and shrugs, "Let's keep driving." And he walks to the door.

"Hold on a minute," I say. There has to be a reason there are no rooms in this state tonight. I ask the clerk. "We've been traveling all day, is there anything you can do? Maybe drag a few cots into the lobby? How about in one of the function rooms? We'll pay whatever."

125

With that, I turn to Flip. It is becoming less and less probable that he will hold on to his hero status through sunrise.

"I'm sorry, I can't do that, you know," the clerk tells us, "but if you tell me what direction you are traveling, I'll check some of our other inns and see if they can accommodate you."

All at once, the three of us say, "East."

Our new destination is Durand, Wisconsin. There is a Holiday Inn with five open rooms. At seventy-five miles per hour we should be there in about one hour. Flip's driving, so we'll get there a lot sooner. Jonathan and I are in the back seat, and he's snoring up a storm. Flip's hands are at ten and two, doing over ninety miles per hour. I don't think he'll blink until we arrive. This road is dead. There are snow dunes piled along the sides from here to as far as our headlights can penetrate the dark. And is it dark. As I look out the window, towards the horizon, I can't tell if my eyes are open or closed.

There are no lights on the road, and no other cars in either direction. No city or town light anywhere. Up in the sky, I see every star ever created—beautiful, shining emeralds against a perfect black curtain. They actually look like they are dancing, maybe a tango. We don't have this kind of sky in Massachusetts, it's never dark enough. There is always some light bleeding in from somewhere. I hardly ever look up at the stars anymore. I think the stars must have become discouraged about the lack of interest from me and my neighbors, and all moved out here. The more I stare, the more I think about how crazy life is. There, above me, are hundreds of thousands of stars. From my limited vantage point, I can scan light-years away.

I can sit here and worry right now about where I'll be sleeping tonight. Or I can worry about my job, or my car, or Tyson Wheeler. I can think back to Janice, or Ranger-girl, or Clint and Charles, or even the guy from the IRS. I can dwell on the fact that I struggle monthly to pay bills and vainly attempt to meet a woman. I can worry that my friendship with Flip and Jonathan is slowly winding down to the point that in a few years a trip like this will be impossible. I can reflect on my first twenty-five years and conclude that I really haven't done much. Or, I can look to the stars and think that one million light-years away, everything I've done, or haven't done, means absolutely nothing. My worries, problems and concerns mean nothing, from the point of view of the guy on a far-off world looking up and seeing my sun.

Everything I've done leading up to this point in my life will set up everything I do tomorrow, and in the future. So with that in mind, why do I delay myself in doing things that can make me happy? Is it because I'm happy with my station in life, that I really believe everything is as good as it's ever been, and should just keep traveling this path? No, the answer isn't that scary. The answer is, I'm afraid. I can confront Clint and Charles because I am a good worker, and what I do, I do well. Neither of them can affect my work. I can go out with Janice, because I've done that before. I can be broken up with Janice, because I've done that before. I can have a fight with a nameless, faceless man from the IRS because I'm as nameless and faceless to him as he is to me. Hell, I can be mean and rude to a woman at the bar and make up stories, because I know I'll never see her again. None of that takes courage. Talking to Ranger-girl would take courage.

What Flip did takes courage. Not just kicking the crap out of someone ten times his size, but listening to his heart and blindly hiking all the way out here, just for a chance at happiness. The eight seconds of intimacy with Dusty wasn't enough to reward him for this journey, but for those eight seconds, I bet nothing else mattered.

Jonathan has courage. I know millions of babies are born every year, but millions of people won't raise their baby, it's up to Jonathan and Dany. For the rest of his life, he'll always be the reason that baby is alive. When he's ninety and the baby is sixty-five, with children and grandchildren of her own, it's all because of Jonathan and Dany. To me that's unbelievable, unfathomable.

In my life, I've always done what's expected. What's safe and right. Well, so far safe and right hasn't made me happy, it's only made me content. Why can't I reach these epiphanies at the train station?

I can't tell you the exact time Jonathan woke up, but I can tell you the reason. His snoring was shaking the windows. I was afraid moose were going to rush the minivan looking to mate. Are there moose in the mid-west? And if there's more than one moose, is it mooses, or mice, or what? I don't know, just as long as he stops snoring. I give him a good smack to the arm.

"Jesus," he says, waking up. "What the hell did you do that for?"

"After sex, do you and Dany sleep in separate houses?" I ask. "How does she put up with you? You snore loud enough to set off an avalanche, if it wasn't so flat here."

127

Jonathan apologizes, then leans forward to get an update on our progress.

"We are about thirty miles away," Flip informs us, "Hey, I have a question for you guys. If Batman met Superman in an alley to hammer out their personal differences, who would win? Superman or Batman?"

"In a street fight?" Jonathan asks. "Superman would. He's Superman."

"No way," I interject. "Superman is too moral. He'd need a reason to fight Batman. What reason would they to have to even fight? He'd just pussy out and walk away. Batman would win by default."

"Are you saying Superman is afraid of Batman?" Jonathan seems offended at the very notion.

"All I'm saying is that Superman with his red, white and blue, truth justice and the American way, would seek the higher ground. And as he walked away, Batman would see a yellow streak on the back of his scary red cape."

Jonathan is fuming, apparently he has quite a hard-on for Superman. "You really think that if Superman and Batman met in an alley with the express consent to brawl, Superman would turn and fly away." He pauses. "From Batman. Who, technically, is not a superhero. He can't fly, he's not fast, he's not indestructible. It's all in the costume, and the car."

I think about this for about half a second. "Ok, fine. Batman may not be your typical super-power superhero, but you can't deny he has super-qualities: he's smarter than Superman, and about a million times braver…"

"Wow," Jonathan stops me, "where do you get off saying Batman is braver than Superman?"

Someone just walked into my super-trap. "Batman has to be braver than Superman because of the very things you so eagerly brought up. He can't fly, he's only as fast as his legs can go, and he is very destructible. When Batman runs into a burning building, a rogue beam could fall from the ceiling and suddenly Alfred is packing up the Wayne manor before it's sold at auction. Superman knows that wherever he goes, he's walking out. Drop a beam on his head, it probably will not even move the super-part in his super hair."

"You know what, make all the little jokes you want, hide behind your sarcasm, you know as well as I do that Batman is nothing more than his costume, and his belt!" Jonathan exclaims.

128

"Ah, it's all in the belt," I agree, "and don't you think that a smart hero like Batman would keep something in that belt just for such an emergency, i.e., Superman goes bad, Batman keeps some Kryptonite inside said belt."

Jonathan does not like this answer. "You cannot assume that Batman has Kryptonite in his belt."

"And you can't assume he is not ready for any circumstance presented at any given time." Now I'm getting a little hot under the collar. "Every time Batman is in a jam, he goes to the belt. What makes this any different?"

Jonathan, holding out his hand, shoots out his thumb, "Superman flies, he's faster than a bullet, which incidentally can bounce off him, and he's incredibly strong." Index finger joins the thumb. "Spiderman can crawl on walls, and is super strong." Middle finger, "Aquaman can talk to fish, and swim indefinitely underwater." Ring finger, "Wonder Woman does that spin thing, and wham, she's changed her clothes." Finally the pinky, "The Flash, wicked fast. Batman has a belt. Wow, I'd feel safe in Gotham."

"Oh, I know, Metropolis is so much better." Now it's going to turn ugly, "One bad guy, Lex Luther. Lex Luther, a man, just like Batman, yet Superman can't handle Lex Luther. What super-abilities does Lex Luther have? Zero. Batman has the Joker, and Riddler, Cat Woman, Penguin, Scarecrow, Dr. Freeze, all scary individuals, who often team up, and still can't defeat Batman. Superman versus Lex Luther, and it's barely a draw. Oh, Lex Luther gives me such nightmares."

Flip jumps into the conversation, trying to re-focus our initial debate. "Okay, Batman and Superman got bad information on one another, and they think the other turned bad. The fight takes place in the desert, away from Metropolis and Gotham. Who wins?"

When Jonathan and I both give our opinion at exactly the same time, and the answer sounded like Batperman. A formidable hero to say the least.

Clearly no agreement will come out of this conversation. Flip continues, "Okay, who would you rather be: Clark Kent or Bruce Wayne?

Again, with the simultaneous answering it sounds like we say Cluce Cayne. I jump in, "Ok, ok, we are getting nowhere. Jonathan, you tell me why you'd want to be Clark Kent, and why you wouldn't want to be Bruce, the stud, Wayne, then I'll give my reasoning why you are totally whacked, and Flip can decide who's right. Fair?"

Jonathan nods, and starts his opinion on the differences. "Clark's a regular guy, from a small town. On Krypton he'd just be son of Jor-El, but on Earth he has these superpowers, yet he still wants to live an un-assuming life. He's a small reporter in the big town, people like and respect him, he's a good guy. He only becomes Superman to help the people of Earth. He's no egomaniac that only comes when you call him, there's no super signal, he goes on his daily rounds, checking out the big city. He gives back to the community that gives him so much. I respect Clark Kent for being unselfish. Batman is ego-driven, and look-ing to score with all the ladies in tight outfits. And seriously, don't you think the Department of Youth Services should investigate his relation-ship with Robin? Come on, he's into some weird sex stuff. Women in leather and young boys."

"Flip," I ask, "was Jonathan cleaning his pants or smoking crack in the bathroom at the bar? Bruce Wayne always gives back to the com-munities, he's always involved in charity work, he gave Dick Grayson a good home. Oh, and what a home. It's a mansion. Where does Su-perman live, an igloo? What's up with his crystal palace? Do you think a date is impressed with stalactites on the ceilings, or Van Gogh's on the wall? Hmmm, tough call. Plus, Bruce gets the ladies, Vikki Vale, Cat Woman, two mighty good-looking woman. Clark Kent can't even get Lois Lane to date him. Kim Basinger, Michelle Pfiffer, or Margot Kidder. Hmmm, tough call. Oh, and Bruce has cars, motorcycles, air-planes, and a butler, Superman has…an igloo. Flip, this conversation is useless, please tell Superboy here who is the best."

"You two both present strong cases," Flip starts. "I'd have to go with Superman in a fight, but Bruce Wayne as an alter ego. Now, if I could be a superhero, it would be Wonder Woman, ohhhh, those legs go all the way up, and she's an Amazon. And all her Amazon friends were so hot. Yup, that would be the place for me."

Jonathan and I lean back in our respective chairs, and leave Flip to his fantasy and the road.

Suddenly, with a bang, something feels like it hit the minivan. It feels like one of those moose tried to go toe-to-toe with us. Flip hits the brakes, while Jonathan and I hang on for dear life. There is a god-awful noise coming from the front of the minivan. I look towards the hood,

130

where the sound is centered, and there doesn't look to be any damage. After a few seconds, Flip has us at a dead stop. He asks if everyone is all right, then steps outside to check the minivan.

"There are no dents, I'm going to check under the hood." Flip says from the cold. A few moments later he returns holding a snake-like object. "I think it's our fan-belt, or maybe the power steering belt."

"Oh shit," Jonathan is about to freak. "Are we going to be stuck here, in the middle of nowhere? How are we going to get home?"

After a few seconds of silence as each one of us tries to think of any other way this trip can suck, I remember that I'm a member of Triple A, and that the first A stands for American. At last check, Wisconsin is covered under American. "Guys, I'll call Triple A, they'll send a truck, no big deal. Flip, do you have your cell phone?"

"No," he says stone-faced.

Now we are screwed.

"Just kidding." He breaks a grin as he leans under his seat. "Here, call."

I call the 800 number, and give the person on the phone all the information we have on our current location and situation. The woman takes the information and tells us it may be an hour or so until she can send a tow-truck. She then tells us to keep warm. No shit.

It's one o'clock Friday morning, and we a stuck on a desolate snow-filled highway somewhere between St. Paul, Minnesota and Madison, Wisconsin. Maybe I actually got killed in the bar, and this is Hell.

When we started this trip, it was full of optimism and hope. Now, as we run home, everything just sucks. We've escaped the fire only to jump into the frying pan, a frying pan that is roughly ten degrees below zero. Maybe it's not that cold, but my goodness it's cold!

Flip, Jonathan and I stand out in the cold, with the minivan's hood up, staring at our fate. Hopefully, Triple A will arrive soon, but it is one in the morning, the day after Thanksgiving. Hours after Thanksgiving. Since the three of us are totally car illiterate, we decided not to try to start the minivan, fearing it'll blow up or something. As we head into the minivan, we are secure in the fact we are currently screwed, again. Jonathan and I file into the back seat, and Flip jumps in third.

"Hey, shouldn't you be up front?" I ask.

"Why?" Flip responds, "To keep the steering wheel company? We have to keep together for heat."

He has a good point. So I sit between Jonathan and Flip, inside a purple minivan, in the middle of the night on a dark desolate road, with nothing to keep us warm other than body heat. Where did my life go wrong?

"How long do you think it's going to be?" Jonathan asks.

"An hour," I assure him. "Triple A is really good. I'm a gold card member."

"I'm a gold member," Flip says in a highly mocking tone. "Maybe if you keep your gold card up your ass, it'll keep you warm."

Wow, a totally unprovoked attack. I'd drop my mouth, but I'm too afraid that it might freeze, and I won't be able to close it again. "What the hell is your problem?"

"You know, Ulysses, I rely on you for only a couple things, and at the top of that list is to keep me from doing stupid things. Today alone my life has been threatened more than once, and you have been at every instance. So now, as the cold hand of death reaches out to the three of us, you just grasp to the hope of a Triple A card." Flip's lit up over something. Even Jonathan looks shocked. I don't think it was too long ago I was the one saying this trip was stupid, and right now I'm the only one with a solution. That's gratitude.

I just roll my head back, and quickly turn to let Flip have it. I'm not in the mood. "Flip!" As I quickly turn, something goes wrong, I catch something just below the belt, and well above the knee. I think a fold in my boxers pulled, and pinched my left nut. It's not that bad, I think I can continue. "Flip!" Nope, I can't continue. "Oh shit, shit." I grab my pant legs, thrust my ass in the air, and hope the nut repositions back to a safe place.

"What's wrong?" Jonathan asks.

I can't answer yet; my testicle is still punching its way through a tour of my bladder. I fold my body and push my forearms into my abdomen. I gently loosen my belt, and put my hand along my beltline. Any tears will freeze immediately upon incarnation.

Jonathan asks again, "What's wrong?"

"Catch a nut?" Flip asks rather uncompassionately.

I nod.

"Boxers: the silent enemy. They are so your friend when you are wearing a suit or dress pants, but put on a pair of jeans and they'll betray you without warning. Snap, you're caught." Flip has such a way. "That's why I wear boxer briefs, the comfort of boxers, the support of briefs."

"I'm a brief man myself," Jonathan adds. "I have one pair of boxers that Dany bought me a few years ago. They're silk. I feel like a porn star when I wear them. They're a little too free for my liking. I need the structure of briefs. I always know where my guys are. That comforts me."

My breathing is slowly returning to normal. I feel the need to massage my abdomen. Slowly I'm returning to myself. Slowly.

"Have you ever got a pimple on your guy?" Flip asks. Jonathan and I turn in shock as to where this conversation is going. "I look down one morning, and there is a little bump. Immediately, I'm wondering who the last lady I had over was, but it had been two, three, maybe six months, so I ignored it. Then, after lunch that day, I hit the head at work, and this thing was so big, it had a personality."

Jonathan and I both grimace. Suddenly I'm not feeling better.

Flip continues. "So that night, I went home and put a warm towel on him. That next morning the white head was as big as a nickel. Well, I had to pop the sucker." I think I'm about to pass out. How can you pop a pimple on your penis? How can you even get a grip on the damn thing? Do you band-aid it afterwards? Dab a piece of toilet paper on it like when you cut yourself shaving? I had to think of something else. How do you calculate a quarterback rating?

Flip concludes, "It hurt like a bitch, but the pressure was gone, oh that pressure was so great. The worse part about the whole incident was for four days I had a little scare/scab, so I put myself on the injured reserved. No ladies, no masturbating." Clearly, the latter was the one most likely to be affected.

"Flip," Jonathan reaches over and sticks his hand in Flip's chest, "I think you've said enough. We have to conserve air."

Flip grabs his hand, "We're cold, not suffocating."

Just then, a light hits Jonathan square in the face. We freeze. The light followed his arm to Flip's hand, then descended down to my open pant button where my hand was massaging my abdomen. The three of us are motionless. If this is Tyson Wheeler of the Minnesota Vikings, we're screwed.

The voice behind the light came booming through the cold and glass. It was a woman. "OK lover-boys, no moving, and pull your pants up. Wisconsin State Police."

Are we saved or in more trouble?

"Do you three know that public displays of lewd behavior are against the law in Wisconsin? Also, do you know that pulling to the side on a major interstate during the winter snow season is a violation of public safety?" the officer states with one hand pointing a flashlight at the three of us, and the other holding the top of her holstered gun. Why did we have to get a purple minivan? She continues to instruct us to put our hands in the air, and for Flip to open the sliding door with his left hand. Within moments, the three of us are outside the minivan, surrounded by the cold Wisconsin night air. "Who would like to explain first?" she says. The name on her badge is Chamberlain. She is young, maybe twenty-four or twenty-five. She has real short hair coming from the back of her trooper hat. A long, thick, warm jacket covers the uniform. She looks like a bitch.

Flip glances over to me with a slight smirk on his face, Jonathan looks at me with a bit a fear in his eyes. I step forward, "Officer Chamberlain," I say as I clear my throat, "our car broke down, and we're waiting for Triple A to pick us up. What you saw in there was bad timing." Suddenly, as the words hit the cold night air, they didn't sound as good as they did when they were still in my warm brain.

135

"Bad timing?" she asked. "Do you want me to come back in ten minutes?"

Jonathan stepped in, "That's not what he meant, I'm married, he," pointing to Flip, "just had sex with a woman not even eight hours ago, and he," now looking right at me, "...he...he well, hurt himself. We weren't doing anything" Oh yeah, that's better.

She steps into the minivan to examine where we have been living out of for the past two days. The smell of egg must still be pretty bad because when she stuck her head in, she immediately pulled it out, then covered her nose and mouth with a handkerchief before going back in. Suddenly, the three of us are aware that the condoms are still in the overhead sunglass holder. Hopefully she won't look in there.

She looked in there.

"Care to explain these?" We just smile at her. "I didn't think so, where are you three from?" Officer Chamberlain asks.

In unison we answer Boston, and Flip goes on to offer more. "Officer, we're out here visiting a friend of mine during her Thanksgiving break. We were heading to a Holiday Inn for the night, then home tomorrow when our car died. I assure you, what you saw inside the minivan was purely innocent," Flip concludes with a wink. In his mind, he thinks he can have sex with her in her patrol car. I hope the jail cell is warm.

"I'm going to my car to check if any service stations received your call. If no one is coming, I'm arresting the three of you. Drivers license, please." With that, Officer Chamberlain sticks out her hand and we give her our licenses. She has us stand in front of the minivan as she steps back into her warm patrol car to verify our story.

Ten very cold minutes pass before she returns. "I'm sorry boys, but your story does not check out. There is not one tow truck in the state of Wisconsin coming anyplace near here right now. Now turn around, I'm going to cuff you until my backup arrives." She motions for us to turn, as she pulls out three sets of handcuffs.

"What are you talking about, I called them myself about thirty minutes ago," I plead. "Check again, they are on their way."

"Not necessary," she says, as cold as the night air. "You boys should know better than to lie to a police officer. Now sit back in your car and we'll wait for my backup. I can't fit all of you in my car."

136

"This is bullshit," Flip screams at her. Jonathan and I try to tell him to calm down. "No, I will not calm down. This has been the worst trip of my life, now you are going to arrest me because my car broke down. You suck."

She grabs her nightstick, "One more word out of you, and I'm going to have to subdue you. Clear?" We tighten our lips. "Now, what's the name of the friend you were visiting?"

Silence. If crickets could live in this God-forsaken cold that would be all you could hear. We look at one another with no idea of how to respond. Do we tell her about Dusty? That might get back to Tyson Wheeler of the Minnesota Vikings. They could come to the jail, bail us out, and then proceed to kill us.

Flip steps forward, "Hrbek," he offers. "We were staying at my friend Kent Hrbek's house. Know him?"

Officer Chamberlain looks at Flip with a bit of contempt. Does she know Kent Hrbek played for the Twins, or is she unhappy that Flip is insinuating she knows this random guy in Minnesota? "Please step back into your minivan, gentlemen."

Flip smiles, and heads into the minivan. Officer Chamberlain closes the door behind us, and heads to her warm patrol car.

Wide-eyed and cold, I turn to Flip, "Kent Hrbek, you jackass. She's going to arrest us just to spite you."

Flip assures me not to worry. There's no way she knows Kent Hrbek.

Jonathan has other things on his mind, "I can't believe this, we're going to be arrested for a late night circle jerk." None of us has ever been arrested before, and to be arrested for this? I can just image what it'll be like to call home. Hi Mom, Dad, the three of us were arrested at one in the morning for giving into our temptations and engaging in long overdue homosexual relations. Where's Tyson Wheeler when you need him?

Twenty minutes passed, and it is so cold inside the minivan. We can see Officer Chamberlain sitting back in her car, and wouldn't you know it, she has a thermos with her. It's probably full of warm coffee. She talking on her CB, obviously about us, and she is laughing.

On the horizon, coming from the east, we can see a pair of headlights. Hopefully it's our tow truck; probably it is the other state trooper coming to take us away. If we are lucky, it's the four horsemen of the apocalypse, and we'll all be put out of our misery.

About a mile before whatever it is gets to where we are, sure enough the sirens go on. Well, on a bright side, in another hour we should be in a warm prison cell.

He is older, probably in his fifties. I'm sure he's not happy about coming all the way out here in the cold to escort three gay men in their purple love shack. He and Chamberlain talk for a few minutes, then they both head over to us.

"What should we do?" Jonathan asks.

"I think we should make a run for it," Flip answers. I hope he stays in his cuffs, I don't think now is the time for his Kung-Fu moves.

"Listen," I say, "we'll go with them, and by tomorrow this will be all squared away. We did nothing wrong."

Flip shakes his head, "We're going to jail. Do you know what they'll do to us three pretty boys in jail? Didn't you see *The Shawshank Redemption*? How about *Deliverance*?"

"Will you shut up!" I scream as the door opens.

"I'm State Trooper Ford, Trooper Chamberlain tells me you three were, well, hanging out where you shouldn't be, and lied to her." He shakes his head rather disapprovingly. "Don't they teach you back east not to lie to the cops?"

I try to tell this guy that this is all one big mistake, but he doesn't care. He shepherds us out of the minivan and towards the two patrol cars. Just as they put Flip in, the cell phone rings.

"That's Triple A," I tell the troopers. "Please just answer it; I'm sure they are looking for us."

Trooper Ford answers the phone, and after a few moments lowers it to his waist. "Trooper Chamberlain, can I talk to you for a minute?"

Flip, Jonathan and I huddle and confer on who we think it is. Officer Chamberlain pulls our keys out of her pocket, opens the driver's side door, and pops the hood. Within seconds, Trooper Ford is on the phone again, and then walks over to us.

"Sorry for the misunderstanding boys," he says, "your tow is on the way." He un-cuffs the three of us, and hands Flip the phone. Then he walks back to his car, mumbling something under his breath. I think he said stupid bitch, but it could have been cupid fish. Either way, I think we're off the hook.

Officer Chamberlain walks towards us, and it's obvious Flip has some comment. "Before you say anything," she points to us, "just know that I was instructed to wait with you, and I can and will subdue the three of you if I feel threatened."

Clearly, she's drinking too much coffee. The three of us just smile, and head back to our car to wait for our tow truck. "Do you want us to contact Mr. Hrbek for you?" she asks.

Flip smiles, hoping Trooper Ford did not hear this. He might not find it funny. "No, we are fine now."

It is a beautiful tow truck, white with red lettering and a big golden eagle on the door. 'Mann Towing and Salvage, greater Minnesota since 1924' it read on the door panel. Greater Minnesota, maybe that's why there were no tow trucks in all of Wisconsin coming. His name is Earl, and Earl quickly becomes our new best friend. Officer Chamberlain drives off once everything looked decent.

"You boys have some sort of trouble?" Earl asks, referencing our police escort.

"No trouble Earl, just the friendly Wisconsin State Police making sure we were not breaking any laws," Flip informs him. "And to be honest Earl, I think she just wanted to get to know me, if you know what I mean."

Earl nods, confirming that he knows what Flip means, which is very frightening, because neither Jonathan nor myself know what Flip means half the time. Earl tells us to jump into the cab, and he'll have us up and running in no time. Inside the cab of the tow truck is a naked lady air-freshener hanging over the rearview mirror, with the hint of vanilla. On the passenger side floor was a Penthouse, and an issue of Time. If he wanted articles, he should get Playboy.

After ten warm, happy minutes inside Earl's truck, he finally steps in. "Which one of you is Ulysses?" I lean forward, and he gives me some paperwork to sign. "That's a weird name, Ulysses, where'd you get that?"

Earl looks pretty simple, so I'll just give him the easy answer. "My parents are big Civil War buffs, and they named me after Ulysses S. Grant."

"I would have thought it was Latin for Odysseus. I'm a big Homer fan." Apparently, people read in Minnesota to pass the long winters. "Anyway, I'll have you back at my garage in about thirty minutes."

His garage? His garage is in Minnesota. That's the wrong direction. That's where the Vikings live. "Excuse me Earl, we were actually heading east, into Wisconsin."

"But my garage is west, in Minnesota," he states as he puts the tow truck into drive, and he makes a u-turn.

"Excuse me Earl," I say again, "we have hotel reservations in Wisconsin, just twenty or so miles east. We have no place to stay in Minnesota."

"That's too bad Ulysses, but my home is west, and I woke up from a sound sleep to come get you boys. The sooner I'm back in bed, the happier I am." Earl isn't budging from his commitment to go west. "Now I can unhook your car, and you can wait for another truck, but I assure you, I'm it for 100 miles."

The mere idea of waiting in the cold again is unimaginable. Jonathan and Flip both look over to me and shake their heads no. We are going back to Minnesota, like it or not. I ask Earl if he knows any place we can stay for the night, and he laughs. "The only rooms you'll find this time of year are at the homeless shelters, and even then you probably have to wait outside." Not the news we wanted. "I'll tell you what I'll do, I'll let you three stay inside your minivan tonight, inside the garage for twenty bucks each. It's not warm, but it's not fifteen degrees either."

"Is there any chance you could fix the car tonight?" Flip asks.

Earl laughs out loud. "That's funny. I like you, you're funny. Now tell me more about that state trooper who had a thing for you."

Flip's not too happy about being laughed at, but he sure doesn't mind telling stories. I look over at Jonathan, and his eyes are closed. That looks like a good idea. I'm asleep in about ten seconds, and the last thing I hear is Flip describing the backseat of the state trooper's patrol car.

In years to come, I won't remember what town we came to, or the street we stopped on. I probably won't remember the name of the garage we ended up in, or the way it looked. I hopefully will forget the smell. Oil mixed with gas, mixed with mechanic BO, and a hint of vanilla. That smell penetrated the steel and glass that was our purple minivan pretty quickly once Earl pulled us into the garage with a huge "Quality Service Friends" banner draped over the front door.

Earl was a nice guy, he took a huge liking to Flip, and I think that made it possible for us to stay here overnight. It's not the Holiday Inn, nor is it the American Inn, but it's fairly warm and safe from the elements, not to mention the Minnesota Vikings.

"Alright boys," Earl opens the door to address us. That smell. "I just set the thermostat at 65, the bathroom's outside the office, the dirty magazines are in the drawer under the socket set next to the pneumatic drill. Don't play with the drill. Oh, and the mechanic will be in around eight in the morning; I'll leave him a note to set you guys up first thing. Goodnight, sleep tight, and don't let the bed-rats bite."

I immediately close the door, Jonathan immediately checks the ground for "bed-rats," and Flip is staring at the drawer under the socket sets next to the pneumatic drill. It's a little past three in the morning. Five hours sleep would be fantastic.

After about two minutes of tossing and turning, Flip starts talking. "Ulysses, sorry about earlier when I yelled, I didn't mean anything by it."

Just as I am drifting off to sleep, Flip apologizes. "No big deal, let's just get some sleep." He insists it was a big deal, and won't be able to rest until I said I accepted his apology. Before he finished that sentence, I say, "I accept your apology." I turn, close my eyes, and start to drift away. Jonathan is starting to snore.

"Ulysses," Flip started again, "Do you believe in God?"

Where did that come from? Does he appreciate that we are fourteen hundred miles from home, and have only five hours to sleep before we have to start driving again? He's asking me about God. The last time I went to church was when Jonathan and Dany got married. I'm not in the mood for this. Maybe if I pretend to be asleep he'll leave me alone. I snort, and sigh.

"Ulysses," Flip persists, "wake up." He shakes me. The son-of-a-bitch shakes me. It's three in the morning, I haven't slept since yesterday morning, almost twenty hours ago. I've been an accessory to vandalism, chased out of the state by the Minnesota Vikings, accused of lewd behavior, and dragged back into Minnesota by a porn-obsessed tow truck driver who is well-read in literary classics. All I want to do is sleep.

"What!" I turn and scream as loud as I can while whispering so not to wake up Jonathan.

"Were you sleeping?"

I'm going to kill him, and feed him to the "bed-rats."

"Yes, Flip, I was trying to sleep."

"Now that you are awake," Flip says, "do you think there's a God?"

I won't sleep until I answer him. I look over at Jonathan, and he's out like a light. How I envy him. "I used to, Flip," I start, "and maybe I will again, but right now, I'm not sure."

This is a new subject for us. Usually the topic is work, or women, or sports, or women who work in sports: mmm, Suzy Kobler.... Rarely, if ever, religion. Probably the closest I've ever come to talking religion with Flip is when I read a passage during Jonathan and Dany's wedding. It's not a subject we avoid, we just have other things to talk about.

Flip turns to me and can't quite understand what I mean, so I have to explain. When I was a kid, my parents dragged me to church every Sunday. I never thought I was doing it to become closer to God, I was doing it to become closer to my folks. We'd go to a morning mass, then get breakfast, and then maybe go to K-mart were they'd buy me an action figure, and I'd play with that straight until the next Sunday. Maybe it was a bit of subliminal bribery, but they were happy, I was happy, and it was all because of church.

Eventually, that routine grew old. Sunday morning mass for us became Saturday night mass. There were no more toys at the end of the tunnel, nor was there French toast and blueberries. Later, when I was in high school, Saturday night became prime social real estate. After a few teen-rage-filled arguments about why do I have to go to church, my parents stopped expecting me to go. I went off to college, and church was the furthest thing from my mind. Occasionally, I'd date a girl who went to church, or wanted me to go with her parents. I'd go, but felt I was doing it for her, not for me, just like those Sunday mornings with my parents.

In my youth I attended CCD, I was baptized, received first communion, but was never confirmed. I did play CYO basketball for three years, even won a championship for St. Margaret's. In all those early years of attending masses and classes, do you know what I remember? The stale bread, the collection baskets, and the uncomfortable seats, or pews, whatever they are called. The sermons were always long, about people and events I couldn't follow. I was raised on television, and every night on TV you watch a story, and each story has a beginning, middle, and end. Then the next week they'd do it all over again. Same characters, different situation. I tried my hardest to relate the sermons in church to stories on TV. Church: starring Jesus Christ as the king, the Virgin Mary as his mother. Guest starring Judas as the betrayer, and God as the almighty. After two minutes of dry, monotone reading I'd go from being focused on the priest and trying real hard to pay attention to distracted by everything and anything around me.

I used to stare at the church, the paintings, the architecture, the pillars and columns, the beautiful stained glass windows. A church, in all its majesty, is truly a beautiful and exciting place, but to fill it with monotone speeches, and then ask for money after delivering stale bread never made sense, nor did it ever get me to want to come on my own.

I envy priests. I envy anyone who can give their life for one thing, one belief. I envy priests in the same way I envy Jonathan, and how he is so committed to Dany. But if you examine the two commitments, I see that Jonathan and Dany want to be together. They want to explore new things in their combined life together, but don't feel threatened when they are apart. Jonathan and Dany do not require me to pledge a loyalty to them every time I see them, nor to each other. The priest, however, welcomes me into his church, and then proceeds to lecture me and tell me everything I'm doing wrong.

What do I mean by that? Church, in my opinion, should be the celebration of Christ and His sacrifice for me and everyone in the world. Is it? I can handle the readings from the Bible. I don't look at the Bible as being a true representation of the time Christ lived. I'm not that naïve. In my short lifetime I've seen history re-written enough times to know a document several thousand years old, with almost as many translations, doesn't stand a chance. The Bible to me is a series of stories that tells us how things should or could be. It's a series of morality plays, sometimes describing a tale where the hero saves the day, other times describing what the hero did wrong, illustrating to us mistakes not to make. Again, it's read poorly almost all the time, they should send those who read from the scripture on Sundays to classes like Speaking-in-front-of-crowds-and-keeping-them-awake 101. Rarely can a priest tell a story and capture my imagination. All those dramatic pauses are less than dramatic. The Bible is full of action, drama, sex and betrayal, but the readings never demonstrate this. Instead they are bland, with no enthusiasm. If I read any of my presentations in speech class like a priest, I surely would have failed. To me, the material is there, but where's the delivery? Now I'm not saying the priest should jump up and down and cry like some TV evangelist, because that might

145

jeopardize their sincerity, but jazz it up a little. Talk to me, not at me or over me.

After the reading, the priest usually speaks for ten minutes about recent issues. He preaches about low attendance, about how the church needs money to send him and some worshipers on a weekend pilgrimage to wherever. He'll note that next month is Vegas night. A church having Vegas night. Have these people ever been to Las Vegas?

The one thing I never liked about the sermons was the way all teenagers were linked together. A common thread of the sermon was today's youth. A priest, in his fifties or sixties, who has forsaken his youth to study and worship Catholicism, thinks he can relate to a teenager. A man who has no children, and only knows about teens through what he reads in the paper or watches on TV has all the answers, based on a two-thousand-year-old book. This priest will tell his parishioners about drugs, and sex, and how a whole generation is being corrupted. He'll say that children need God, and guilt parents into bringing their kids to church. He's playing to the demographics: parents 25-50, with children age 4-12.

When I became a teenager and went to church, suddenly I felt very uncomfortable because when the priest said that teenagers were troublesome, filling their lives with drugs and sin, he was accusing me of this very same stuff. Who the hell is he to accuse me and my friends of such things, and in front of my parents no less? I was an honor roll student, who never did drugs, nor did I hang out with kids who did drugs. I wasn't having sex, as I mentioned before, bad skin saw to that. I took offense at being lumped into a minority, one that he saw as reflective of a whole generation.

Now, I still hold harsh feelings towards religion. Whenever I attend a wedding or a funeral, I hope in some way that priest will speak to me. That he'll say something that will make me forgive the narrow-sighted priests of my youth. That maybe things have changed, and the stories are delivered with flair, the songs are sung with passion, and the sermons are thoughtful, intelligent, and lack ignorance. This may be a bit selfish, but I want to a sermon that speaks to me, and could relate to my life, and help me answer my questions.

But that doesn't answer Flip's question. Do I believe in God? Maybe if I grew up in a different neighborhood my perception of church would be different, but my perception of God remains fixed. I like to think there is a God, but I'm not sure. Not a yes, but not a no either. A definite maybe.

Two thousand years ago there was no question about it. God created Earth, and Heaven, and we go from one place to another after death where we are reunited with everyone and everything we ever loved. But what if that huge asteroid that wiped out the dinosaurs never hit the Earth 65 million years ago? Would humans ever have existed? Would God have created man, or would Darwinism have won by default, and instead of being evolved from ape, man might have evolved from dinosaur—if man ever existed at all. If God created the Earth, why did he wait two billion years before he plopped man here, and why did he wait another sixty-five thousand years before anyone gave him credit for creation? And why waste all that time with the dinosaurs?

Faith in God as an adult is a little like faith in Santa Claus when you are a kid. Kids believe in Santa so much that when Christmas comes and there are presents under the tree addressed from the man himself, how can you doubt his existence? But later, when you learn the truth, you start to ask how you ever really believed in a fat man in a red coat that traveled the world in one night to give away free toys to good girls and boys. Furthermore, if Santa could get everywhere he had to in one night, why does it take me three hours to fly to see my grand-parents in Florida? Why hasn't the military raided Santa's sled hanger and exploited the secrets of his mind-blowing speed? Why, if Santa has elves to make the toys, are they wrapped in boxes that say Hasbro and Kenner? I was disappointed when I found out there was no Santa Claus, but in reality the man affected my life one day out of the year, and the first year without Santa I still got everything I wanted for Christmas, the only difference being my parents finally got their due credit. What happens the day people find out there is really no God? What happens the day they find out there really is a God?

When things are bad in my life, I pray to God. I ask God to help me find an answer. When things are good, I thank God for any intervention he may have had. Does it help? I don't know, but it doesn't hurt. I also carry around a lucky rock, I don't know if it helps, but it doesn't hurt. My parents are such believers, which carries enough clout that I just can't dismiss the possibility. But the way I want to recognize Him is not the same way the church wants me to. In my opinion, just His acknowledgement should be enough. God is not vengeful nor spiteful, so if I thank him in my own way, He should have no problem with me skipping church.

Finally, I took a moment to myself, to think about my theology. I got pretty deep for three in the morning. "Flip, what do you think?" I turn to the son-of-a-bitch, and he's sleeping. I just bored him to sleep. Wait—he's sleeping. Jonathan is sleeping. I can sleep. Thank God.

Her lips are sweet, like a fresh pear on a hot day, full of moisture and passion. Her hair is perfect, wrapped in a braid behind her head with only a few, daring strands joyfully dangling in front of her eyes. As the lights hit her face, her red lips leap out and smack my senses. She moves effortlessly like a cloud dancing in front of the sun. I extend my left hand to meet her right. Palm to palm, I gently pinch her fingers and lead her into me. A cold chill runs up my back, as her heat crashes into my chest. The lights are dim, the music is low, and this is my moment. With my right hand I cradle the back of her head and pull those red lips closer.

Never before and never again will a kiss mean so much to me. As I dip her ever so gently back, I ask my Ranger-girl what she's thinking. She smiles, opens her mouth, closes her eyes and snorts, "Knughh." I shake my head, I don't understand. My eyes can't focus on her anymore. My moment of passion has been temporarily interrupted. I'm furiously blinking to regain my vision. There's her hair, there are the lips…my God, it's Janice. "Knughh," she snorts again, "knughh." What is this? Where's Ranger-girl? What's happening? I look out to the crowd of people that has gathered around us, and it's actually a perimeter of squirrels closing in on me from every direction…"Knughh!"

You can imagine my relief when I woke up and found my snorting ex-girlfriend was none other than Jonathan wrestling with comfort in the back of a purple broken-down minivan in the middle of nowhere Minnesota. The disappointment is also a little high, knowing that Ranger-girl's lips were too a fantasy.

My watch says 4:15. Wow, I've slept for about 30 minutes. Well, I'm ready to head home. A quick jab to the ribs, and I get Jonathan to stop his snoring. I look over to Flip, and somehow he's still asleep. I need to sleep. I'll just sit back, relax, and will parts of my body to relax, and ultimately sleep. I will my toes to relax. I will my feet to relax. I feel the relaxation flowing over my body, up to my calves, and my knees. I will my legs to relax, and fall asleep. "Knughh."

If I break his ribs it'll mean a hospital visit, and we'll have to stay in this god-forsaken frozen glacier of a state that much longer. I have to draw down deep inside my soul, and just fall asleep.

"Knughh." 4:45. The last half hour has taken a week. I'm absolutely exhausted, but every time I come close, Jonathan and his fog horn reach into my subconscious and rip me from entering slumber. I've passed the point of caring if I break his ribs, right now I have to be careful that I don't kill him.

"Knughh," 5:05. In the time it takes the second hand on my watch to move 1/60th across the face, I can recite every word from my high school commencement address, play back in my head the last episode of Cheers, Seinfeld, and M*A*S*H, figure out the square root of 149, and hypothesize what the secret ingredient in Coke might be. Why won't he stop snoring?

"Knughh," 5:19. The night before my birthday and the night before Christmas were a lot like this. My parents would feed me a big meal and keep me up late past my bedtime, hoping to wear me out, but it never worked. No matter how tired I was back then, I woke up every twenty or thirty minutes to look at the clock. I was that much closer to the payoff. Sleep was just in the way. I want to sleep! "Stop fucking snoring!" I scream at Jonathan, grab his arms, and plead into his chest. "Please, stop!"

Well, it looks like emotion got the best of me there. Oh look, Jonathan has woken up.

"What?" he says as if he has no idea. "What, I'm awake, what?"

"You were snoring," I inform him, "and I couldn't sleep. Why do you snore so loud? It's torture."

"Sorry, Jesus," Jonathan says, "all you had to do was nudge me." Oh, he thinks that's so easy.

Flip leans in, "Are you guys hot, I'm going to turn down the heat." It is a little hot, maybe that's what is keeping me up. I turn to Jonathan to apologize, but the bastard has already turned over and fallen back asleep. Flip jumps out of the minivan, turns the heat down, and runs back in. Let's try this again; I can still get close to three hours of sleep.

5:48. I'm awake. Jonathan is not snoring, Flip's fine, what woke me up? Could it be the constant shaking of my limbs? Jeez, it got cold, real fast. I guess a garage with three bay doors doesn't provide a lot of insulation.

"Ulysses, are you awake?" I hear from Flip's way.

"Yeah, I'm really cold. Can you turn the heat back up?" I ask.

150

"Good idea," Flip opens the door, and runs towards the thermostat. I look over to Jonathan, and he's out cold, literally. Flip's fumbling with something. I can't quite make it out, but he's definitely trying too hard to turn up the heat. He finally comes back, "I think I turned the heat down too much before, and accidentally turned it off, and now I can't turn it back on. There must be a shutoff switch so they don't waste heat." I could ask him to repeat that, but it would do no good, I heard him the first time.

"Shit."

We've woken Jonathan from a deep,

loud sleep and the three of us try to make a plan on how to stay warm until 8 o'clock. It's only a little more then two hours away, but it's so cold in here even the girls in the dirty magazines are covering up. Each one of us has looked at the thermostat, first Flip, then Flip and I, then Jonathan, then Jonathan and Flip, then all three of us. The only way we can get heat out of that thermostat is if we light it on fire.

"Well, this is just great," I start, "is there anything else that can screw us on this trip? I think we have to face facts: we are never leaving Minnesota. We will die here. Most likely this morning. If the cold doesn't do it, the goddamn Vikings will." I start pacing, looking throughout the garage bay for something, anything. What will I do when I find this something, I don't know, but finding it is the first step. I think Jonathan and Flip are starting to worry about my sanity.

"Ulysses," Jonathan walks towards me, "It's not that bad, sure it's cold, but in a couple hours, the mechanic will be here, and we're on our way."

I'm not comforted. All I can think of is the end of the movie *Titanic* when all those frozen people were bobbing in the water. Is that how they'll find us? Hell, we'll probably have to huddle for warmth, freeze to death, and be found by the morning mechanic. He'll call the cops and report that he found three gay men cuddling to death inside their purple minivan. The papers will probably call our deaths a lover's pact. Not very fair. I guess that state trooper in Wisconsin will be happy; I can see the smug look on her face right now as she sings, "I was right, I was right."

Well, I'm not going to let that happen and without warning I find the something I was looking for. Actually, it's a somewhere; I call over my lovers, as I'm sure the press would have referred to them as. Too bad that now they won't have the chance. A plan is forming. "Look, across the street." I direct them to an oasis across the street. A bakery. But not just any bakery, one with smoke pouring out of the chimney, and light glowing from the back of the building.

"So," they both offer.

I guess some people just can't appreciate a lucky break. My grandfather used to own a donut shop back when I was just a kid. The only things I remember from his shop were the smell and the warmth. When I was seven, my grandfather died, and over the next few years I slowly learned more and more about the man. He died of a heart attack at the age of sixty-four, relatively young. He'd been a baker his entire life: pastries, donuts, cakes, anything that required fat, he produced. He used to keep tubs of grease and lard, two major ingredients every recipe could not have enough of. Well, when I was seven, my grandfather was an old, tired, beat-up sixty-four, and time took him. As it turned out, a diet of lard, along with working twelve- to sixteen-hour days for forty years, will age a sixty-four-year-old man well before his time. The relevant information here is that bakers work long days, producing fresh pastries primarily for morning consumption, in a warm location.

"Gentlemen, we will cross the street, volunteer to help that poor baker for two hours, eat some of his booty, return for our minivan, and leave this hellhole." I don't even wait for a reaction. I head to the minivan to gather my wallet and my toiletry bag. I figure if I'm going to surprise a total stranger by volunteering to help him bake, I should comb my hair and brush my teeth.

"Ulysses," Jonathan grabs my arm, "you can't be serious, we're exhausted. We can't do work right now, and besides, he'll probably think we're psycho and call the cops."

I shrug him off, "That's fine, prisons are heated," and maybe I can get a cell away from Jonathan and his snoring. There is absolutely nothing that will stop me from this course of action. This is the first real idea I've had this entire trip that will benefit the three of us. If they could just see things as clear as I can right now. It is as if my grandfather is directing me in what to do. This will work.

As I turn from the minivan with my toiletry bag to face the bathroom, Flip is standing in front of me, "Ulysses, hurry up, I want to freshen up before I go over too." We exchange smiles, and I hustle to the bathroom. Things are going to work out, starting now.

The plan is simple; we'll cross the street, knock on the door, present ourselves to the owner, and offer to help, asking nothing in return other than warmth. If I know bakers, he'll be glad to have the help. I look over at Jonathan and Flip, they are all smiles, very professional. I think they're buying into my plan. This is going to work. I knock.

154

The hours of operation are 6 AM to 4 AM, but there's a note on the door, "Opening at 7 AM Friday after Thanksgiving." I knock again. A face pops out from a window behind the counter. He says something, and shakes his head no. Clearly he doesn't know the opportunity presented to him. I knock again. This time the man (late forties, head full of gray hair, or is that flour, and a big white apron from head to toe) comes to the closed door and screams, "We're not open yet." He points to his watch, then the door, then turns. I have to be more persistent. I knock again.

I think I might be aggravating him now. He walks to the door, and screams through the glass real slow, "I am closed." I try to tell him we're not interested in food, and he snaps back, "No beggars." With that, he closes a shade in my face. I turn to Jonathan and Flip a little set back, but not yet dissuaded from my goal. I knock again. Nothing. One more time. Silence.

"I guess maybe I was wrong." I turn and say to my friends. At the same time, I see a figure come from behind the corner of the building. He's holding a gun.

"Now I figure you ain't burglars because you haven't made a move yet, and you can't be beggars, because there's nothing here for you, so what do you want with my store?" Normally, a man pointing a shotgun at me at six in the morning would worry me, but right now, it seems like the natural progression of things.

"Sir, hi, my name is Ulysses, this is my friend Flip, and this is my friend Jonathan." They both wave and smile on cue. "Our car's broken down across the street, and we have a couple hours before the mechanic arrives, so we figured we have time, we'd like to help you out."

I think due to sleep deprivation, my powers of persuasion have suffered. The man with the gun and flour in his hair smiles, laughs to himself, puts away his gun, and walks to the back of the store from where he came.

The three of us stare at each other for a long minute and continue to shiver. That was it, we have nothing left. This looks like the end. I think deep down I always knew Flip would lead me to my death, but I never thought I'd give up so easily.

Then I heard it—the most beautiful sound I've heard since the last time Ranger-girl sneezed on my train. It was the sound of a deadbolt being unlocked, and a door opening. "Where are you boys from?"

"Boston, sir, we were on our way home when our car broke down, and Earl brought us here," I inform him.

"Where does Earl keep his porn?" he asks. Jonathan and I immediately look to Flip. This is the test to judge the validity of our story.

"Under the socket set, next to the pneumatic drill, sir," Flip answers. If he had answered that confidently on his SATs, he'd would have had his pick of Ivy League schools.

"If Earl told you that, then you must be ok. Come on in boys, my name is Dan," he says as we enter, "let's get you out of the cold."

Dan talks to us for a few more minutes to size us up. We reiterate that we are just looking for a place to pass the time and stay warm, and that we'd do some work in return. After showing us his morning operation and pouring us each a cup of hot chocolate, Dan hands Jonathan a broom, Flip a mop, and me a dish rag. Nothing too glorious, but it's warm in here.

I remember when I was younger my dad

would tell me stories about working in his father's bakery as a kid. Free donuts and free hot chocolate. He was the envy of every ten-year-old at Keith Elementary. He said his dad would just load him up with donuts for all his classmates; a sure way to make friends. Dad used to tell this story that years ago, his father was approached by this crazy inventor who had this idea to automate the donut process; to press the donuts from a mold, thereby increasing the output exponentially. Well, gramps didn't go for it; he thought people wanted their donuts handmade, with care and love, not manufactured using a cookie cutter.

To make a long story short, the bakery was not around long enough for me to take any freebies to school. Incidentally, one of my grandfather's competitors did buy into the mass donut assembly line idea. From what my father tells me, this competitor was Dunkin Donuts. Can I prove it? Maybe, I'd just have to do a little research on the origins of Dunkin Donuts. In all honesty I have no proof as to my father's claims, but it's a good story, we keep it in the family, and we hold no grudge against Dunkin Donuts. It's all for the best; why would I want to be known as the prince of donuts, heir to the kingdom of jelly and lemon?

I don't know, but I bet I'm inside this warm bakery because grandpa is smiling down from heaven, helping me and my friends out.

No sooner do I put the image of grandpa in heaven in my head then I remember the conversation I had just moments ago with Flip. I guess in some ways God is there when you need him, or we just lucked out that Triple A called this garage.

Jonathan has pushed his broom close to me, "U, is this why you were so against this trip from the get go?" he asked. I smiled and got to cleaning my cookie sheets. Jonathan took another step closer to me. "We've been friends for a long time," he starts, "but we never have deep conversations about stuff."

I don't know what brought this on. "What are you talking about, Jonathan? We talk about stuff."

"Stuff yes," he says, "but not Stuff. Not life and death…and God." Why does everyone want to talk to me about God today? At this time of the morning? "Do you really believe those things you told Flip back in the car about 'maybe' there is a God?"

I was just quote-mimed by one of my best friends. You know, when someone opens their arms, closes their fist, then extends two fingers on either hand only to squeeze them with every syllable repeated from an earlier statement you made. "Maybe." Well, I must have hit a button. "Jonathan, I really didn't say yes or no to him. I more or less left it open for interpretation. It's just my opinion, that obviously you do not agree with. No big deal, but weren't you sleeping?"

"I'm creeping up on the first anniversary with my wife who's pregnant for the first time after a miscarriage, and I'm stuck in nowhere Wisconsin."

I correct him, "Minnesota."

"Does it matter?" He's right, it doesn't matter. "Anyway, do you really think I could sleep inside a minivan, smelling like eggs, with two guys I just escaped with from an angry mob? That wasn't sleep, that was my body trying in vain to get my mind to subscribe to the same train of thought."

"Dude, I heard you snore."

"Okay," he submits, "maybe I dozed off for a second or two, but I heard everything. Anyway, I just wanted in on the conversation, but with Flip around I knew it would not go too far. I think he fell asleep somewhere around when you said you'd go to K-mart for toys.

"Here's my take, there has to be a God, or has to have been a God, because without the hope of something more, than what's the point? Why tease us for a cosmic second, if we can't love forever? Everything under the sun needs love, and something had to implant that feeling into our souls. Without love, man would have lasted one generation. He would have looked at woman and said, 'hmmm, whatever'." Jonathan made another mime-quote. "And what about bravery?"

"What about bravery?" I ask.

"If the fireman, policeman, soldier, or even terrorist did not think there was a God, do you think they would still risk their life? Almost every religion promises an afterlife. If that afterlife was not true, would people be so willing to die for a belief or cause? The afterlife is the safety net to bravery." Jonathan has a good point. If this is it, if we have a finite existence, would anyone be so willing to lay down their life, and end everything they have, without being able to rest forever in Heaven?

158

A New Odyssey

"Then why does God let bad things happen?" I ask, "Why is it that He will sit back and not stop a terrorist attack, or a fireman from running into a building that is clearly about to collapse?"

Jonathan grins as if he's about to deliver an answer he knows I will not like, but one that he might not like himself. "God gave humans their own free will and therefore made us responsible for the consequences of our actions. He is not in the business of 'why.' It's not 'why' did God do this, rather God is in the 'how' business. Man might be cruel to man, so we should turn to God and ask him 'how' should we deal with something. How can we get over, and move past, or grow from an event that man caused onto himself."

"So you are saying that God is a spectator to mankind, bumps and all," I conclude.

"I'm saying that God planted the garden, now he lets it grow. In every garden you have weeds, and in every garden you have life blooming as well." Jonathan pauses for a second. "It's up to each one of us to grow, and avoid the weeds of life."

I look over Jonathan's shoulder and see Dan peeking over at us. As I grab another cookie sheet, I motion to Jonathan to sweep this general area around me so we can continue to talk. "Jonathan, I'm not debating that, and you make a beautiful point. All I want is some kind of proof."

Jonathan stops me and asks, "Ulysses, when something is bothering you, and you are alone in your apartment, and you talk out loud, who do you think is listening? Do you ever feel better afterwards? I'll bet you do, because whether you like it or not, God's listening. And I think you know that."

I never knew Jonathan felt this way; I guess the private sessions with Reverend Rivers did do something for him after all. He's not being a fanatic about it, and I don't get the impression he's trying to convert me. He's just being sincere, and what he says, if true, is great for him. "How about this, you and I and Flip all believe in God; well what about the guy in China who thinks it's all about Buddha, or those middle-easterners who are all into Allah? If we are right, they are wrong. If they turn out right, where does that leave us, purgatory?"

Jonathan smiles, "At North Union who's Phil Gelenian? Who's Leo Mann? What about Kathryn Forrester?"

I'm on vacation, besides weren't we talking about God? "Phil's the top dog, Leo's the CFO, and I think Kathryn is in charge of commercial banking, or something. So?"

"This is how I see it," Jonathan starts calling out names and counting them off with his hand, "Phil, in North Union terms is God, Leo can be like Jesus, and Katerina can be Allah. Why can't Heaven be like a company? God is the CEO, and all his direct reports, like Jesus, follow a common agenda through different means. The goal for all of them is to get us to Heaven, but there is just some intra-office turmoil. Have you ever seen when they put the manager of the IT department in a room with Kathryn? All they do is fight over who's more important, but their goal is the same—a common agenda as prescribed by North Union's God and CEO Phil Gelenian."

Interesting perspective, but what does that all mean to me? "Jonathan, that sounds convincing enough, but I need more. I don't care if some almighty omnipotent being looks over me, listens to me, guides me; I care about why I am here, not if He is here. Don't you ever wonder what the big picture is? Why are we here? Why do some guys live decades on the streets hustling for change while others cure cancer? What's the value of any one person's existence compared to anyone else? Sometimes I just can't help but think what it would be like if I was never here, or who's going to care when I'm gone." These words sit in the air for a few moments until Flip rounds the corner. Jonathan and I grin as if to call it a draw and Flip walks over to us.

"Hey guys, I was wondering," he says thoughtfully, "Is a tomato a fruit or a vegetable?"

Before we can downshift into Flip talk, Dan the bakery owner screams from the front of his shop. "Holy shit, no!" Must be bad news. We go running out to see what's wrong with Dan as he is leaning on his counter with the newspaper spread across it, the floor, and against the window. Did someone cancel the one day of summer they get around here every year? "The goddamn Vikings did it again. Wheeler and Johnson-Harris both got jumped at a bar and early reports say they might be out for the rest of the season. Jesus Christ, you know, they only get paid a billon dollars to work from August to January. Why can't they just stay out of harm's way…why damn it why?!?"

Dan is clearly upset by the almost certain end of the Vikings season. I step towards the counter and reach for what might be the sports section, "Does it say what happened to them?" Oh, please don't say what happened. We'll have every Viking redneck on our tail from here to Boston, if we ever leave.

"No," Dan informs us, "it just says that they were jumped by a bunch of guys at a bar. Reportedly Cowboy fans. Damn Cowboy fans. Your team can't make the playoffs fairly so you do a 'Tanya Harding' on our fine boys." He mime-quoted 'Tanya Harding,' is it something in the morning air? "Are you boys football fans?"

In unison, "No." Sometimes it's like we rehearse the timing of this stuff.

It's 6:50 AM, just over an hour until the mechanic gets to the garage. I can't wait to get out of Minnesota. The three of us walk back to our respective jobs and let poor Dan lament until his 7 AM crowd filters in.

At 7:55 Dan hands us a box of donuts for our trip and one coffee for the garage mechanic. We thank him for the warmth and hospitality, and tell him we hope everything works out okay with the Vikings. Secretly, I think the three of us are becoming closet Cowboy fans.

The mechanic, Al, turns out to be a really nice guy, although he is clearly upset about the current fortunes bestowed upon his Minnesota Vikings. Is there anything else to do in this state other than following the Vikings?

Earl told Al about us, and he fixed the minivan so we could get on our way by 10 AM. Flip had to lay down almost two hundred bucks for the repair, and ultimately Al ate most of our donuts, but by 10:30 we were back on the road, and past the scene of our earlier breakdown. Next stop home.

It's a beautiful clear day, so Jonathan and I volunteer Flip to drive; we want to get home fast. Flip wonders aloud if we ever thought we would be on our way home. I just smile and nod, Jonathan closes his eyes and says he never had any doubt.

This strikes me as odd because on several occasions in the last twenty-four hours Jonathan has looked very worried. I ask him if he is serious and he informs me that he has to get back home to remove the evidence.

"What evidence?"

In a very tired voice he says, "Whenever I go away on a trip without Dany, to insure my safe return I plant some incriminating evidence around the house that she would find if she were going through my personal things in the event of my death. That way I have to get home, and remove the evidence so she does not think any less of me." This sounds more like Flip than Jonathan.

"So what did you leave out?" Flip asks.

"I left a Playboy, tissues, and some hand lotion by my computer in the basement." Jonathan has a smile on his face that I can only describe as warped. "Dany goes nowhere near the computer. She hates the basement. She would only go down there if she was forced to by circumstance. So, if I return home in a timely manner, I never have to worry about her finding anything. Therefore I'm always encouraged to get home when I'm expected."

I don't know what is funnier, the thought of Dany finding the Playboy and lotion, or choirboy Jonathan buying a Playboy at the store. I bet he spent fifty bucks on cigarettes and batteries before he even asked the clerk behind the counter for the magazine.

The trip home was very uneventful, thankfully. We came to the conclusion that a tomato is both a vegetable and a fruit. Flip insisted that a tomato is a fruit, because one can eat a tomato plain, it grows above the ground, and is not green. Jonathan and I argued that it is a vegetable. Vegetables go in a salad. Vegetables are sliced and put on a hamburger. No one would ever slice an apple or orange and pop that on top of a cheeseburger. We went back and forth for three hours. Finally, we reached the compromise after stopping at a Subway on the inter-state. Flip had a salad and said that by our logic, bread must be a vegetable because it goes in a salad as a crouton, and goes on top a bur-ger, as the roll. We asked Flip if he ever had a fruit salad, and how many tomatoes were next to his grapes and watermelon. In the interest of friendship we called it a draw.

We drop off Jonathan, and at about five in the morning, Flip pulls into my apartment complex and drops me off. We had rotated the driving re-sponsibilities several times on the trip home, making sure Flip got the odd shift, requiring him to drive a little further than Jonathan or myself.

I'm sure I will look back at this adventure favorably some day, but for now I want my pillow and my bed. I hope little Jack is still in his cage. If I have to go looking for that reckless rodent right now, I'll die from exhaus-tion. Sleeping in a minivan, no matter for how long, is not restful. In less than five minutes, if all goes well, I'll be asleep. This is heaven.

"Ulysses," Flip reaches out his hand for me to shake it, "thanks for doing this. It was fun."

"It was interesting." I shake his hand, and I even agree to go with him tomorrow when he goes to return the minivan. I have to help him validate the story about why it's missing a rearview driver's side mir-ror. It's amazing when you hit a hole in the road how easily those things can just pop off, and how quickly you can make up a lie to save a few bucks. "See you around noon."

As I turn to walk away, Flip still has my hand. Maybe he doesn't realize it; maybe he just doesn't want me to be asleep in four minutes fifty seconds. Maybe he's being an ass.

"Ulysses," Flip looks at me as with a glimmer in his eye I rarely see—sincerity. "Yesterday morning at the bakery when you were talk-ing to Jonathan about God, I was listening, and though I'm not the poster boy for any religion, I don't think you should be so cold towards it."

Flip offering me an opinion, on religion no less. As bad as I want to be asleep in four minutes and thirty seconds, I'm so fascinated by this.

"Flip, I'm not being cold towards it, all I was telling Jonathan is that it doesn't speak to me like it does to others" He releases my hand.

"Do you want to know what I think?" Flip asked.

Tough question. Sure I'm interested, but it'll delay my sleeping plans. I'll tell him we can talk about it tomorrow, all day if he wants. I just want to sleep. I take a deep breath, close my eyes, and pucker my lips to push out the 'F' sound in 'Flip' just as he starts to tell me…

"I know you are tired Ulysses, but think of this." As Flip starts, I know I'm too weak to stand and hear this, so I resume my seat inside the minivan. Flip begins, "If we are only here, together, for tops seventy years, what harm does it do to hope that someday, when life ends here on Earth that our soul goes to someplace like Heaven? My grandparents used to tell me that in Heaven I'll see my mom again. I'll be with my dog Sarge, and their dog Co-Co. I'll be with them again. Even if it is only a trivial hope, every time I think of it I can't stop smiling. I never knew my mom, and to finally be able to hold her…I…"

For a moment I see Flip's eyes well up. I'm not thinking about sleep any more. I reach out my arm and place my hand on his shoulder. He looks up and smiles.

"Sorry. See, I am sensitive." Flip wipes his eyes. "I really believe this. And if religion is true, if Heaven is there, then it's eternal. And do you know what the great thing about eternity is? It has no end and no beginning. So if Heaven is eternal, and my mom is there right now, then she's not waiting for me. I won't just show up after I die here on earth, I'm already there in Heaven with her, and she's holding me."

"My grandparents are there, my kids and grandkids are there. They have to be because time, in Heaven, doesn't exist. So there is no end to the joy."

I think my eyes are about to well up. For Flip, this is unbelievable, and beautiful. How did this guy who has always been out in left field ever put this kind of scenario together? This is not the Flip I know. I remove my hand from his shoulder, step out of the minivan, lean into the open window and again say my goodbye.

"And one other thing," Flip offers. "Do you know who will care if you were here or not?" There's a pause as I wonder how long was he eavesdropping on Jonathan and I at the bakery. Flip finishes, "Your friends will."

I really can't say much else because Flip just blew me away. I smile and head towards the stairs that lead to my apartment; Flip rolls down his window to yell yet one more thing to me.

"Oh and Ulysses, every woman in Heaven has huge tits." Flip cups his hands in front of his chest in an attempt to show me just how big those tits in heaven are. Pretty big.

Now that's the Flip I know.

I walk in the door, check on Little Jack—he's there, though plotting I'm sure. I have two messages blinking on my machine. Almost everyone in the world I care about knew I was in Minnesota for Thanksgiving, so whoever is on the machine isn't that important to me right now. They can wait until I wake up…whenever that is, you know.

Have you ever seen the movie *Jaws*? Not

Jaws 2 or *Jaws 3*, and definitely not *Jaws 4*, but *Jaws* the original. Three guys on a boat, hunting a shark. They go out on the water, throw some chum to attract the shark, then over the span of two days they hook him, shoot him, poke and blow him up. That whole scene where the *Orca* is sinking, Hooper is presumed dead, and Quinn just became a Stoffers entree was pretty intense. Brody, leaning in the crows nest, aiming for the shark. Hoping to hit that can of compressed air and blow up that damn fish. The shark is swimming right for him, fins a-blazing, then ka-boom! Brody hits the air tank and there are little pieces of shark everywhere.

Well, right after that Hooper shows up and he and Brody kick to the shore using a floating barrel. End of movie. When they finally get to shore, after two long grueling days battling a giant fish, losing their boat and captain in the process, how do you think they felt to be home, and have that ordeal behind them?

Those two days in a small boat must have seemed more like two months. Three men in close quarters battling the elements of nature. Life-and-death situations around every corner. Nothing going the way it was planned, but it all worked out in the long run (except of course for Quinn getting eaten). How do you think they felt to finally get to the shore, get home, put their heads on their pillows in the safety of their own houses?

I'll tell you how it felt: damn good. I slept all day Saturday from the time Flip dropped me off until Sunday morning. No waking up to go the bathroom, no rolling over to get more comfortable. After three days of living in a minivan, I could have slept comfortably on a bed of hot coals. At least the coals would not be moving, and I would not have Jonathan or Flip on either side of me snoring. I'm close with my friends, but I don't ever have to be that close again.

I don't even think I dreamt, which is something I cannot say too often. I am so rested right now, I feel like I could conquer the world. Of course, the odds that a situation will present itself in the next few hours that would permit me to conquer the world are pretty slim, so I'll just be happy with the knowledge that if I had to, I could.

The final box score for the trip was slightly in our favor. We were 3 for

3 in fast escapes, 11 for 12 tossing eggs, but 1 for 3 in the sex category. Other stats included disabling not one but two large Minnesota Vikings, evading arrest for lewd homosexual ménage-a-trois behavior, and breaking the Boston to St. Paul speed record (if indeed there was one.)

The near-killing and the smell of egg scored against us, but all and all we came out on top.

Flip insists he should get credit for two items on our top ten, sleeping with a celebrity and punching Bryant Gumbel. Jonathan and I insisted he does not get credit for punching Bryant Gumbel, but we might bend the rules regarding sex with a celebrity. Not so much that Dusty had any celebrity status, but that sex with her resulted in news in a lot of papers.

Little Jack looks as if he might be a little mad at me. My parents came over and fed him while I was gone, so he's not hungry; maybe he just missed me. Sure, and maybe I'll let him free—I don't think so. However, his wood chips need to be changed, so maybe that's his gripe.

While LJ runs on the floor inside his hamster ball and I clean his cage, I remember I have two blinking messages on my machine. I walk over to the machine, hit play, and head back over to LJ's cage. The electronic voice starts:

You have two new messages. Friday, 4:50 pm:

"Hi Ulysses, it's Kristen from work. Donna and I are going in on Sunday, around noon. Could you call the security desk so those two jerks will leave us alone? Thanks, see you Monday."

Jeez, no. "I hope you had a nice Thanksgiving," how rude. What the hell do they do in the office that they need to go in during a holiday weekend? It's not like we need to work more then forty hours a week; actually, I have a tough time finding forty hours of work to do every week, not that I'd tell anyone that. Hell, I'm the hardest working man in the world. I silently smile to myself as I think about that. Hardest working man in the world. If that were true, it would be an easy world to conquer. Anyway, if I'm having trouble looking busy for forty hours, well, what the hell are these two doing?

The electronic voice continued, *Friday, 10 pm:*

"Hi honey, it's Mom. Your father and I just came back from your apartment, Little Jack was happy to see us. We gave him food and water, but your father said you can change the wood chips yourself. I think he's afraid of Little Jack. Anyway, we saw that your refrigerator was a little empty, except for all the beer. I hope you are not drinking too much. So why don't you come over for dinner sometime this week. Call us when you get home. We hope you had a wonderful trip. Bye bye.

"Oh, your father was wondering if you could bring home his Civil War Chess set. He's going over your uncle's Sunday night, and they want to play chess. I'm going shopping; the excitement of those two playing Civil War chess all day might be too much. OK, bye bye."

To mom, brevity may be the wit of knowledge, but not when it comes to voice mail. The longer, the better. Where the heck is that Civil War chess set? Holding a bag of hamster poop in one hand, and a wet rag in the other I look around my apartment for a sign as to where my father's Civil War chess set is. I remember borrowing it because no one I knew believed that somebody actually bought it off of TV. I think it is at work. Jesus, if he knew it was in an unsecured location, he'd have my head. Like I said, I'm named Ulysses after Ulysses S. Grant, Union General and eighteenth president. My parents met at a Civil War convention in Washington, D.C. My father's grandfather was the son of a Union soldier who lived with a former Confederate soldier up here in Boston after the war. That soldier turned out to be the great-great-grandfather of my mother. How they ever figured this out is beyond me—just as long as they aren't cousins. So as you can see, if I lost any piece of this Civil War set, then I'd have no respect for my parents or my family's past in their eyes. I guess I'm going to work today.

I'm not going to call work for Kristen or Donna. Screw them, why should I have to go out of my way because they cannot do their job in the time provided? Not to mention I did not get a Happy Thanksgiving from them on the voice message. Maybe I should put them on warning? That would be cool, but it wouldn't solve anything. But it would be cool.

I called my mom. Dinner is at seven o'clock on Tuesday, but I'll bring by the chess set after the Patriots game this afternoon. She's going to make chicken on Tuesday; I ask her if she needed me to bring anything, she of course said no, but I told her I'll pick up a case of beer.

Flip's coming around noon, and the Patriots are not on until four o'clock; they are playing the Dolphins today, so we have plenty of time. After I follow him to get rid of the purple minivan, we'll have to drive into work to get the chess set. He won't like it; he doesn't like going to work when he's not scheduled. That's why in the morning it's all about bagels, coffee, and muffins. There shall be no work before it's time.

At 12:30, I hear the horn. I grab my car keys, head out the door with a bottle of Coke and a granola bar. I wave to Flip as I jump in my car. It's been four days since I drove her last. Oh, that's too long. I turn the key, rev the engine—240 horses through eight cylinders sounds so sweet—and pull out behind Flip. The minivan, our lifeboat for four days, looks so different now. It looks battered and beaten. I guess twenty-eight hundred miles in ninety-six hours will wear anything down. At least I got to take a shower this morning.

Flip walked into the rental office with a

story. He was just casually driving along the highway, fifty-five miles per hour, hands at ten and two, when we hit an unexpected bump and the mirror just popped off, obviously due to a manufacturers defect. He'd been rehearsing this story ever since Tyson Wheeler of the Minnesota Vikings inspired him for the tale.

Flip was ready for a confrontation. If the dealer didn't believe him, Flip would make a scene. His go to line was going to be, "Are you calling me a liar?" Credibility is big to Flip. Actually, the illusion of credibility is big to Flip, and if some rental car dealer—a guy who rents cars, not being good enough to sell cars—insinuates Flip is a liar, well then, Flip will let him have it. How dare they say Flip is responsible for damage to their car? The bump he hit in the road is responsible. Of course they don't know that bump is named Tyson Wheeler, but why do they have to know that?

So we are in the office, Flip hands the rental agent, Brian, the keys, and starts to square the bill. Some old guy grabs the keys, goes out to the car to check it out, and seconds later walks back over to us. He says to Brian, "I think we have a problem with the purple minivan."

Brian excuses himself, and follows the older guy outside. Flip's nervous, but he's been ready for this. He's practiced. He's run the drill in his head. He closes his eyes, and concentrates on the story. I step back.

Brian returns, "Excuse me, Mr. Paine, we have a slight problem with the minivan."

Flip jumps right in, doesn't blink, turns bright red in the face, and spits out in a monotone voice even Robbie the Robot would be ashamed of, "I was driving at two and ten, I mean ten and two at fifty-five...fifty-five miles per hour and it fell off. I mean I hit a bump and it happened. I didn't do it. I'm not lying."

Brian seems confused. "I'm not calling you a liar, Mr. Paine, I just have a question about the condition of the car. What happened?"

Quickly Flip answers, "I was just driving...good."

"Mr. Paine," Brian tries again, "there seems to be a prevailing odor inside the car. We just want to know what was spilled so we can treat it."

Flip stares at Brian for a moment. I'm standing a few feet further

171

back thoroughly enjoying myself. I wonder if Flip will egg himself. Flip out of the corner of his eyes, leans his head up, puts one hand on his hip, and reaches toward Brian with the other. "Oh, you see, what had happened is my friend, um, sat on an egg, got the egg on his pants, then fell in the minivan. You might be smelling egg."

Brian smiles, "Piece of cake, we'll treat that and clear out the smell. I will have to request an additional ten dollar payment from you, but the smell will be lifted out of the fabric. You might want to give some of this treatment to your friend." Brian has a nice way about him. Flip looks out to the parking lot; the old guy is driving the minivan around the back of the building.

Flip runs his fingers through his hair, leans back against the counter, and says, "I thought you were going to ask me about the driver's side mirror." No sooner did he say that then he realizes he should not have.

I take a couple more steps back, just in case. Brian steps behind the counter, "Oh that, just figured you hit a bump. Those things happen all the time."

Flip smiles, signs his receipt, and we both leave as soon as possible.

"Are you going to mention the power steering belt?" I ask.

"No," Flip said as he jumped in the car. "No, I think I'll chalk that up as paying my pittance. I kind of got off really easy this weekend, I figure too easy. If a broken belt is the worst they can throw at me, I'll take it."

Good point; after all, he did have sex with a twenty-year old PR major from the University of Florida while her huge professional football player boyfriend finished his turkey and cranberry. Not to mention he kicked said football player's ass. Better a broken belt then broken face.

As we drive out of the rental dealership I turn to Flip and ask him if he minds driving to work for ten minutes so I could get my father's chess set.

"No way dude, I got to watch the pre-game show. I want to see if I'm mentioned for slaying the Wheeler giant."

They are not going to mention him. I need to get to work. "Flip, it's my car, I'm driving. I'm going to be there ten minutes…"

He cuts me off, "Ulysses, I got to watch it. What if they show Dusty?"

There is a silence in the car. After the weekend we just had I'm ready to blow up on the guy. Why is he one of my best friends? Why do I put up with this shit?

"Ulysses…" Flip turns to me. "OK, let's go to work, your dad's stuff is more important then a girl I'll never see again."

That's why I put up with his shit. Because he is my friend, and he puts up with my shit. "There's a train station by the mall," I say to Flip, "I'll take the train in, and I'll call you when I leave work. By that time the pre-game will be over, and we should be back in time for the half-time show."

"Thanks, Ulysses."

"Thanks nothing," I turn to him as I drive, "I'm lending you MY car. So help me God, you better drive it like it is MY car. Not yours, not a rented minivan, MY car." MY thumb hurts from poking MY chest every time I say "MY." "Oh, and watch out for any bumps that might damage MY mirrors."

It's only been four days since I was last at work, but as I stand in front of the Monrow and Midder building it feels like years. How much have I aged this weekend?

It's a very quiet day in Boston; there were about four people on the train with me, and I passed another four or five walking here. And it's not like we have a foot of snow on the ground. It's fifty degrees outside. How many people are watching the NFL pre-game shows?

A swipe of my badge, and I'm in. Only Charles at the desk right now. Clint must be doing his rounds. Charles and I have no relationship at all. Like I said, he hardly ever talks. When Clint has a problem, Charles stands right behind him with flashlight in hand.

The elevator is only a few feet past the security desk. From the door to the elevator I keep my head down until I just get to the desk. I look up at Charles and throw him a slight smile when he stands up and calls out my name.

His voice is the definition of raspy. How long did he smoke for? I stop and turn, all along reaching out, feeling around, and hitting the elevator button. Charles rises from behind the desk, and walks over to me. This is odd—we never, ever talk. He's probably going to be pissed at me for not clearing Donna and Kristen, let alone myself. Why are the elevators so slow here?

"Your name is Ulysses, right?" Charles asks. I'm actually close enough to read his name tag: Leo. He looks like a Leo.

"Yeah, can I help you?" I ask.

"Son," he starts, "this is not an easy thing to do, and I've had to say it far too many times in my life." I raise my brow as he reaches into his pocket to pull out a handkerchief. "Thomas, the other security guard, passed away Thursday night. He had a heart attack while staying over his daughter's house for the holiday."

Leo pauses momentarily to compose himself. These guys were obviously close. Suddenly I feel like a total ass. His head drops down a little as he uses the handkerchief to wipe his eyes. I reach out my arm and try to place my hand on his shoulder. No sooner do my fingers hit his padded security jacket shoulder when he pulls his body back, lifts his head, smiles, and sniffles.

"He was a good man, fought in two wars. I served on the police force with him for fifteen years. I'm going to miss him."

I'm shocked. Clint…Thomas seemed so strong. Wednesday he looked great. "I'm so sorry, sir," I say to Leo.

"He liked you, he thought you were funny. A few months ago you said something to him that sent him back in time to a place he tried desperately to forget: North Africa, 1944. He had a friend, a buddy, that he swore up and down was the kindest man God ever created. I guess this kid had a gift that no matter how hellish the land was, he always knew how to keep his friends and platoon mates together and unified. Sadly, he stepped on a mine while out on patrol one morning with his unit. Thomas said part of him died that day too, and it took years to get over that death. Thomas was one of those men who never spoke of the wars he fought and the battles and blood that surrounded him for so long, but he spoke of this kid. This teenage kid that could dig into a foxhole with you for a week and make you feel like everything would be fine, that each bomb was the last. A few months ago you said something to Thomas which flooded back all those memories. I am sure you did not even know it, but you made an old man remember that he should never forget. He said you were a dead ringer for this guy."

The elevator dings in the background. I'm just standing there watching Leo. I don't know how the react. Though I think these guys take their job way too seriously at times, I actually looked forward to my morning exercise. I just kind of stare off, just to the left of Leo's right arm.

"Your elevator is here, I don't want to keep you, but hold on one second, will you." Leo turns and heads back to the desk.

I turn, step halfway into the elevator, and hold the door-open button. Leo returns and holds out his hand. "I don't think Thomas would mind if you had this. It's his buddy's dog tags. This was his lucky charm, I don't know how there is any metal to it still, that old fool rubbed it every day constantly. He said it reminded him of the strength one man can emanate. I guess his buddy had a saying, telling anyone he would run into to live for the moment, live right now, because you might not get another chance to experience right now again."

I reach out my hand and Leo drops this silver-pressed dog tag and chain in my palm. It's old, the edges are a little tarnished and dented in, and the bottom is worn pretty well. I look up at Leo, "Did Thomas get to experience right now again?" I ask.

Leo grins from ear to ear, "All the time."

The elevator door closes and I just stare at my gift. Valentine, Donald P. is the name with a serial number and a home town of Greensboro, North Carolina engraved. Just holding this thin, warm dog tag feels awkward. I don't even know if I deserve to hold it. In sixty years, only two men have been responsible for this thing. I don't consider myself in the league of World War II veterans, let alone one that sacrificed his life. It is kind of an honor though. From Donald to Thomas and somehow it ends up in my hands. If only this thing could talk, I can't imagine all the history trapped inside it.

The elevator doors open up and I head out to my desk, looking down into my hand as I hold this dog tag. I must be in some weird funk because all I can do is concentrate on this dog tag. I get to my desk, sit down, and look up when suddenly I hear a thud from the copier room. I jump up and run over to the copier room entrance. It sounded like the ceiling caved in. Just as I get to the door, Kristen pops out and stops me. With a hand in my chest, she tells me everything is fine. She looks rather surprised to see me.

"Like Hell it is, what was that noise?" I ask. She presses my chest harder as I try to peek in. Who the hell does she think she is? I grab her arm, lifting it off my chest and moving her to the side. I wrinkle my brow at her as I walk through the door.

The Grand Canyon at sunset: that is a sight. Mt. Everest's peaks: that is a sight. The eruption of a Hawaiian volcano: that is a sight. Donna trying to pull up her jeans, which are clearly two sizes too tight, while lying on the ground next to a knocked-over copier machine: that is THE sight.

"What the fuck!"

Kristen steps in front of me again. Her eyes are the size of grapefruits. "Ulysses, it's not what you think." Donna is now on her knees and the jeans are practically on, her long t-shirt covering any indecency.

I turn my head and look down at Kristen, "It's not what I think?" I lean right in her face, "What the fuck!" I might be breaking some human resource protocol in my choice of language, but come on, what the fuck is going on here. And for Kristen to tell me it's not what I think, well I'm thinking some pretty wild shit right now, and even if it is not what I think, it's still some pretty wild shit.

"Kristen, you push me in the chest to prevent me from seeing Donna half-naked next to a pretty expensive piece of equipment smashed on the floor. If I don't hear an explanation within one second then it's obviously what I think."

Donna steps forward, "Ulysses, it's like this, we saw a mouse run behind the copier, I leaned over to get it out from behind, and the whole thing fell over."

"Why were your pants off?" Donna looks to Kristen, then to me, then to Kristen again. I point at my eyes, "Hey Donna, right here, why were your pants off?"

After a slight hesitation, Donna tells me that she feels a little over-weight, and likes to loosen her jeans when she's alone. I rub my eyes, and walk over to the copier. There is glass everywhere. "Why don't you two see if you can find a dust pan and broom around here." I lean down and try to upright the copier without shredding my hands. Kristen and Donna walk out. I'm tempted to ask them if they are all right, if they got hurt or cut, but why should I, I don't really care. This is not what I need right now, and definitely not what I needed to see.

I get the copier upright, and the poor thing waddles once back and forth until it's perfectly flat on the ground. The front door swings open. I close it but it only swings open again. The frame must be bent because the door is not hitting its clamp to close. I squat and start pulling the door down, hoping to get it back into its clamp, when I see a piece of paper jammed in the mechanics. I reach in and gently pull out the paper. It's a photo copy of what must be Donna's ass because Kristen's profile is right next to it with lips perched outward. Interesting. I fold the paper and put it into my pocket. I'm going to enjoy calling Dwayne Monday morning and giving him his job back.

I lean up against the printer, fold my arms in front of my chest and wait. Why didn't Flip come with me, this is better than any football pre-game show.

Donna enters the room with Kristen right behind her, which I'd expect based on the picture. In the most caring voice I can muster I say, "So are you two ok? Donna, do you want me to call an ambulance?" They both provide me with a blank stare. "I saw some little black

178

specks back here, it could be mouse droppings, I wonder how many run around this place while we're out during the weekend. Disgusting, isn't it?" Though I never got into acting after college, when I need it the training kicks in and I can turn it on.

"So you believe us?" asked Kristen.

"Why wouldn't I?" I reply. "Come on, let's all get out of here." As I walk through the door with the two "girls" I stop and reach into my pocket. "Oh, and by the way," I unfold and hold up the picture, "what the fuck?" I say in a much different voice.

I really don't have a mean bone in my body, but these two had it coming. I quickly fold the paper again and stuff it in my pocket. "The way I see it, I can call security right now and have you both kicked out, never to return, or you can both grab your things, casually walk out, and never return. I'll take care of the termination with HR tomorrow morning. OK?"

There was another blank stare, then the water works. Tough shit, I saw Dwayne when these two went on their witch hunt, I mean bitch-hunt, maybe they should have been nicer lesbians.

After I stand by and watch Kristen and Donna get a few personal belongings out of their desks, I escort them to the elevator, and down they go—away, evil ones! I step to my desk, dial security, and ask Leo to get their ID badges because they have been fired, for all intents and purposes. Leo asks why, and I tell him they did not have authority to be here today, and they destroyed North Union property. Leo informs me he hears the elevator door ding, and he would take care of the problem.

I can just imagine it. The door opens and Leo is standing there with his flashlight. Kristen trying to mask her tears, and Donna trying to figure out a way to make me look like the bad guy. Leo will stop them, using his flashlight as a toll gate. He'll ask them for their ID badges, and after Donna argues for a moment or two, Leo will put her in a submission move, drop her to the floor, his knee in the back of her head, and take the badge.

Kick ass, Leo.

Next I thumb through my Rolodex. Such a primitive database, but very reliable, and I look up Dwayne Martinez. I figure I'll leave him a voice mail, and tell him I have a couple openings in my group, if he's interested.

Finally, I call Flip. I tell him I'm taking the 1:15 train home, and

179

that he should meet me by 1:45 at the train station. I tell him he should have come in with me, that he missed the most amazing thing ever. He asks me if I caught Kristen and Donna doing it. I told him what I stumbled upon was better, not that finding those two engaged in carnal discovery would be good on any level. He's dying to know, but I said he had to wait, because he did not want to come in with me.

I then asked him if my car was ok. He laughs and hangs up. I guess I could call him back, and after a quid pro quo, both our questions would be answered, but I'd rather see the look on his face. Besides, if he had damaged my car, there is no way he'd answer the phone. He'd be heading back to Minnesota, where he'd be safer dealing with the likes of Tyson Wheeler of the Minnesota Vikings, and not me.

What an interesting day this has been.

By the time I got to the train station

I was a little out of breath. You see, I had to run a great deal of the distance because I forgot to actually grab the chess set I came in to find. I was so emotionally drained from the copier incident, and seeing Donna's ass, not to mention the death of Thomas, I had a lot on my mind.

So I had walked out the building, and walked halfway to the train station when I realized I forgot the chess set. I ran back in, up the stairs to the third floor, to my desk, then back down and out. Leo watched me through his monitors at his desk. As I ran out, he said I looked fast. I think I have a new buddy.

I get to the train with about a minute to spare, sit down right in the middle of the car, put the chess set on the floor between my legs, hunch over and place my head in my hands as I catch my breath. I'm so out of shape.

I open my eyes, and peek at the floor through my hands. The train is dead. I can see only three other sets of feet. Two sets to my left, sandals with socks, and old running shoes. And to my right, tiny little Reeboks.

As the train pulls away, I'm jostled into the seat, and feel a pinch in my left pocket. I reach down and pull out the dog tag. "Donald P. Valentine," I say to myself. The name means nothing, but the tag has an indescribable feeling about it. A presence that feels almost comforting. Thomas held this thing for all those years, and though I did not know him, I feel his warmth around me. The more I think about it, goose bumps pop up all over my arm. So now I have a good luck rock and a motivational dog tag. Damn good thing no one has ever given me an inspirational bowling ball. Imagine the back trouble I'd have lugging that everywhere. I wrap the dog tag in my fist, then push it into my pocket.

"Ah-chewwww."

To my right, tiny Reeboks sneezes furiously, and, being the polite young man my mother thinks she raised me to be, I look up to bless the tiny Reeboks. I have the "G" sound for God all set to pass my lips as I look up to bless my fellow commuter, when my brain quickly identifies who it is: Ranger-girl. Before I know what is happening, instinct takes over. Years of training kicked in. The words must have been taxiing for take-off, and did not wait for air-traffic control to clear them to leave. I must have zoned out utterly and completely for two seconds as my brain absorbed the fact that I was ten feet from Ranger-girl. She looked at me and said "Thank you," so I must have blessed her, I just blanked out during it.

Pull it together, Ulysses! "You're welcome," I reply. I can feel my tongue chickening out on me and running to the back of my throat. I'm struggling to compose myself. It's just me and Ranger-girl. Ten feet apart, and I just blessed her. What a great day. I ask myself why I haven't gone to work any other previous Sunday.

"Thanks," she smiles again at me, and puts her head down, thumbing through a magazine.

"Oh, you are welcome," I say with a large smile, but just before I can continue by telling her I was happy to do it, something in my head stopped me. 99% of me is not currently thinking; thank goodness that one percent still working controls the over-anxious idiot button. How much of a conversation do I really think I can muster out of a sneeze?

Oh man, is she looking good today. Straight leg blue jeans, frayed just above her Reeboks. A black leather biker jacket with a cute red and green scarf. She has her hair tucked into a knit Red Sox hat. She wears Red Sox hats; damn, she's incredible.

"Ah-chewwww! Ah-chew!"

"God bless you," I quickly say. After all these months I finally get to bless her, which brings up another question, why does she sneeze so much? "Wow, that's two. One more and I'm going to have to charge you." Suddenly I'm aware that the one percent of my brain controlling the aforementioned over-anxious idiot button just fell asleep on the job. I smile, roll my eyes, and turn away.

"You know," she starts, "I've been taking this train for months, and no one has ever blessed me. Thank you." She speaks with such sincerity, eloquence and education. Ok, now I have to say something smart. Keep the ball rolling. Build from this moment. Be a man.

"Yeah…"

That's it. Yeah. I suck. Come on brain, help me out. What would Gary Cooper do right now? What would Tom Hanks do if that was Meg Ryan? Shit, what would Flip do? I'm desperate.

The moment has passed and it's too late to continue. I need some-

182

thing to start again. Maybe she'll sneeze. Come on Ranger-girl, sneeze. Why isn't she sneezing? Dust. I need dust. I can't just whip my hand on the floor and hold it under her nose, I need to be subtle. If I grind my foot into the floor, that should generate some dust. As I start to grind my foot, I realize it'll take a week to generate enough dust to carry ten feet to her. Damn it, this sucks.

Suddenly, I feel the train slowing down. We're two stops from where Flip's going to pick me up. Please, don't get off. I need a little more time. I need a plan.

The train stops, and three teenagers get on. They sit directly across from me; to the right of Ranger-girl. There are a hundred seats on this train. Why do they have to sit here? As the train starts off, Ranger-girl sneezes again. One of the teenagers blesses her before I can. She thanks him, looks at me and smiles. Oh, we are such a polite train. That fifteen-year old jackass just intercepted a sneeze meant for me. I smile back to acknowledge that she just got a second person to bless her on one train ride, after months of rudeness. That son-of-a-bitch.

I dig into my pocket intending to pull out my lucky rock but instead I pull out the dog tag. I slip the chain through my fingers for a few seconds just as one of the teenagers yells to the others, "Come here, take a look at this." The other two stand and walk over to the windows by one of the doors. We must be riding next to a billboard of Britney Spears. I turn to see what they are looking at: nope, no Britney, but it got them away from Ranger-girl. The next sneeze is mine.

The train starts to slow again. Please do not get off. I just need a break. As the doors open, the three teenagers get off, and Ranger-girl keeps her head down in the magazine.

One more stop. I've got about five minutes. I might never have an opportunity like this again. I'm totally psyching myself out over this. Look at her. She's beautiful. She must have a boyfriend. How can I be so naive to think she doesn't have a boyfriend? I raise my left hand to my forehead and tap myself over the brow, as if this action might assist me in my planning to sweep Ranger-girl off her feet.

"Ouch," I say quietly to myself. Forgetting I still had a steel dog tag in my hand, I whacked myself in the forehead. Donald P. Valentine. What would he do right now? What would Thomas do? Leo said Thomas used the dog tag to motivate him to live in the moment. The "right now" as he said. What if right before he went to war, Donald P. Valentine was on a train, saw a girl, but didn't talk to her because he lacked the courage? What if he thought he could try to talk to her after the war when he came home? What if just when he stepped on that land mine he thought about that girl, and the missed opportunity of his life?

What if I just walk over to her and say hi, my name is Ulysses McHugh. I close my eyes, take a deep breath, and try to relax. As I open my eyes and look at Ranger-girl, an overwhelming calm rushes over my body. The light pours in from the train windows and cascades across the floor. I stand up, put the dog tag in my right pocket, and walk over to Ranger-girl.

"Excuse me," I interrupt her reading. "Hi, my name is Ulysses McHugh, and I just wanted to come over here and introduce myself to you." I hold out my hand.

She reaches for my hand, "Hi Ulysses, I'm Audrey." She cocks her brow, "Do I know you from somewhere?"

Yeah, my dreams. "No, I've just seen you a couple times on the train, and I just wanted to say hello." We let go of each others' hands. She has soft skin, and long fingers. Her whole hand fits right in the middle of my palm. I'm not too sure if I just shook the hand that caught any of the three sneezes, and I don't care.

"Well, it's nice to meet you," she says with a smile.

"And it's nice to meet you, Audrey." I smile and turn back to my seat. The train is slowing down; we're at our stop. I lean over and grab the Civil War chess set off the floor. Audrey walks up behind me as we both walk out the door together. I stop to let her go first.

Flip's standing in front of my car holding a big poster-board that reads "Single White Male looking for meaningless encounter." All I need is for Audrey to see me walk over to this moron and think I want part of his meaningless encounter.

"Look at that guy," Audrey points to Flip, "what a creep."

"He sure looks like one," I say.

"Well, nice meeting you, Ulysses," she says as she turns to walk away.

"Nice meeting you, Audrey." I smile as she slowly turns and takes a few steps. "Audrey," I walk towards her.

She stops and turns, "Yes?"

"Would you be interested in having a cup of coffee at Charlie's with me tomorrow before the train?" That's as courageous as I get.

184

She smiles, looks down to the ground, and pinches her lower lip with her right hand. "How's quarter past seven?"

"Sounds great," I confirm. Suddenly "Celebration" by Cool and the Gang is blasting in my brain.

"Then I'll see you tomorrow. Have a great night." She turns and walks away.

I can't get the smile off my face. Now's that's a good "right now." I silently thank Thomas and Donald. I can almost see their ghosts appear before me with big smiles across their faces. Just like the last scene of *Return of the Jedi* when Anakin, Ben and Yoda appeared before Luke. Same exact feeling, same exact moment.

I look over to Flip and he hasn't made eye contact with me yet; I bet he was hoping for a bigger crowd to embarrass me even more. I pretend to walk over to the newspaper dispenser as Ranger-girl…as Audrey drives away in her Volkswagen Jetta. She has a Red Sox license plate on her car. This girl rocks. She waves as she drives by, and I wave back. I cannot wait for tomorrow.

With Audrey clear, I walk over to Flip. With a strong lisp he yells, "Oh, a man, a man. Want to take a ride in my car, handsome?" I knock the poster board down, throw my right arm behind him and my left hand over his mouth as I plant a kiss to the back of my hand covering his mouth.

"You're the man of my dreams, take me away," I say, pushing him as far as I can.

"OK, Ulysses," he says as I let go, "I know I'm hot stuff, but think of our friendship." He hands over my keys and wipes his mouth, just to make sure there is no trace of my saliva on him. "Who was that girl you were waving to?" he asks.

"That was Ranger-girl," I inform him, "Her name is Audrey, and I introduced myself. We're having coffee tomorrow."

"Huh." Flip's reaction was rather low-key. "Now aren't you glad I made you take the train?" I don't know what I was expecting from him, I was thinking he'd put me up on his shoulders and parade me around the parking lot maybe. That was Ranger-girl! Does he not know how monumental this very moment is? That was Ranger-girl! Flip reaches into his pocket and pulls out a business card. "Hey, I found this in your backseat," he says. What was he doing in my back seat? "This girl has cute hand-writing. Do you mind if I call her?" I look at the card and I see the name: Maria Crane.

"All yours Flip, oh, and the e-mail is 'likesantamaria', not 'thesantamaria'."

I grab my keys, and we both get in the car and drive away. That night the Patriots beat the Dolphins 24-13. The next morning Audrey and I had coffee at Uncle Charlie's and took the train in together. We had a wonderful conversation, and wouldn't you know, that guy I saw her with is gay. Dany is right, finding happiness should be a top ten item to a fulfilling life. Hell, it should be #1. That night we took the train home together as well.

You know, that was easy, simple.

Printed in the United States
84362LV00006B/132/A

9 781595 267078